the housewives of greensea island

Julie Farley

FOG HOUSE
PRESS

Fog House Press

ISBN: (Paperback) 979-8-9997695-6-5

ISBN: (E-book) 979-8-9997695-5-8

Cover design and illustration: Jen Colburn Design

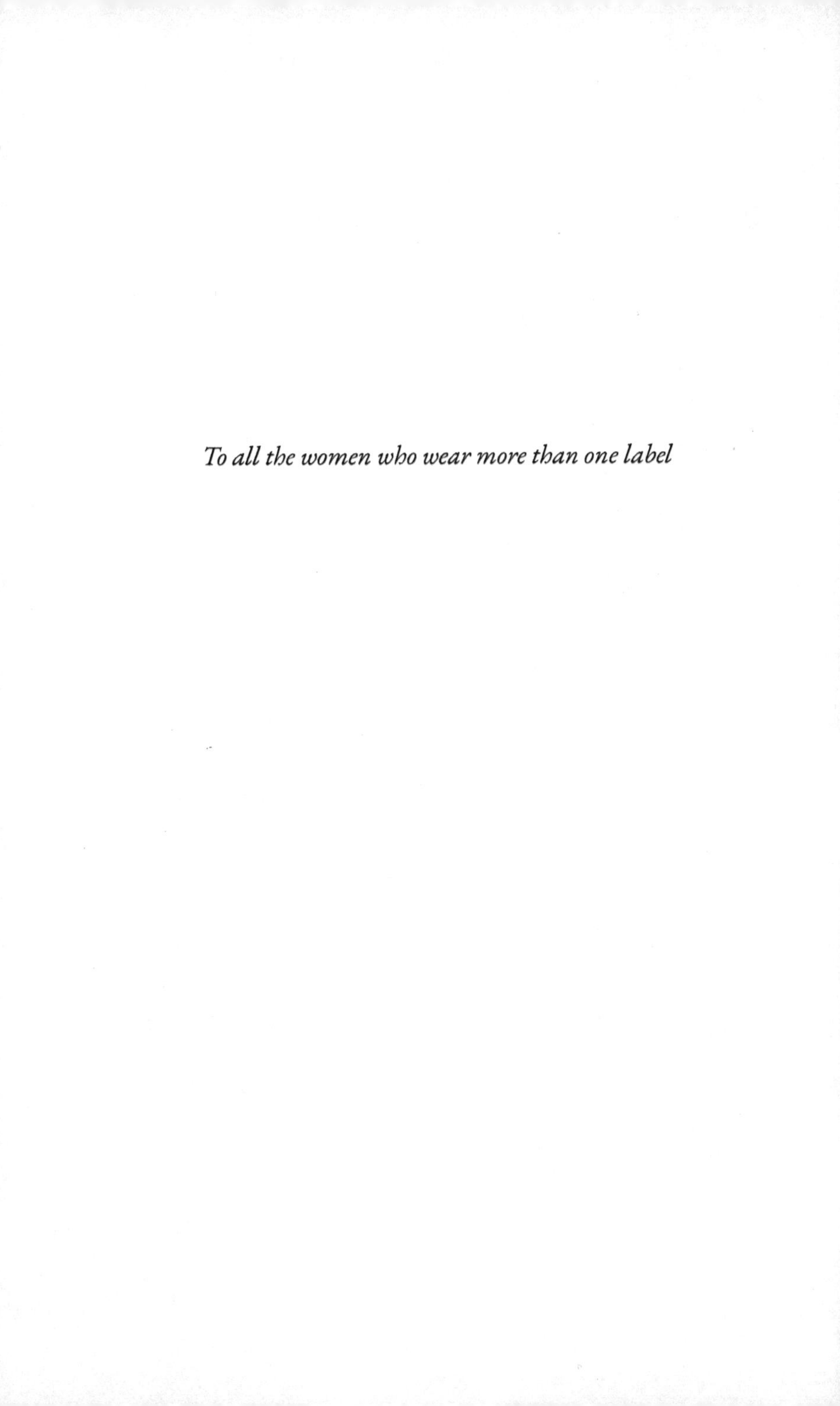

To all the women who wear more than one label

greensea gazette

Islanders,

Let me set the scene...

It's just another day with the foghorn blasting for the always late 5:45 ferryboat as it glides into Grays Bay. Oh, today is a little different because the sun came out and is now poised to slip behind The Brothers—the most prominent peaks of the Olympic Mountains.

The newly installed roundabout continues to bewilder (instead of welcome) bikers, pedestrians, and cars as they disembark the ferry. The mayor's created a mandatory e-course for all island residents to learn how to properly navigate the oversized cement circle, while longtime islanders pine for the days when traffic lights weren't passé.

And tonight, the hum of gossip lingers across the island like a heavy fog.

Greensea-ers wonder why an emergency town meeting has been called. Has someone painted the Greensea Goat the wrong shade of white—again? Are they ready to harness the tides to run the ferries on tidal power? Never...imagine that fiasco, scheduling the boats along with the tides. High tide or low tide for the 7:05? Or, perchance, a well-designed collection of tiny homes designed to meet the need for low-income housing? Gasp. Could Greensea be so forward thinking?

Sports practices will end at the buzzer. Carpools will run like an Olympic event. Meals will be thrown together with the efficiency of a fast-food restaurant—but make it organic. The usual suspects will swing by Thin Pines Country Club for a quick check-in with their golf bros to see if anyone shot a course record while they had their nose to the grindstone in the city. But most commuters—with questions twirling in their minds—will traverse the windy, tree-lined roads to arrive home. All while the rest of the island rushes their evening routine as they prepare to assemble to hear about the latest threat to their blissful island lives.

In other words, don't be late. It's important, and you know the mayor likes to start on time. And remember, if you can't make it, I'll be livestreaming.

xoxo,
GG

the mayor who cried wolf

Laura Prescott

The last time Laura Prescott attended a town meeting, she left with a new client after Mayor Nickerbottom declared pickleball part of the island noise ordinance, making it illegal before 8 a.m. The plastic pop of the ball apparently echoes across the bays. Laura does not have time for another client, or tonight's town meeting.

"Jo, Meg, no *Love at the Last Resort* for George while I'm gone tonight, okay?"

Laura asks her rhetorical question as she drops her keys into her purse. The girls nod from the sectional without taking their eyes off their phones.

"Come on, Mom! It's getting good!" George pleads as he stands in the center of the family room on the balance board her ex got him.

"Nope, not till you're double digits," she says, hoping he'll forget well before then. She kisses him on the head as he wobbles from side to side.

Laura treads over to the sink and grabs the compost bin to

empty outside as she makes her way to her car. She's contemplating giving up on her save-the-Earth antics to cut one more thing off her household chores list. But the soil in her flower garden next to the front door will reward her for her efforts in early summer.

Standing in the driveway, she breathes in the fresh Greensea scent—eau de saltwater and pine.

The plastic lid sticks as she attempts to tip the compost bin. Something scurries from the bushes along the driveway, and Laura jumps back, losing her grip and sending the compost spilling across her and the dormant garden.

Great.

She removes carrot peels from her jeans and a piece of apple peel from her sneakers. Smelling like rotten fruit and vegetables at the meeting is not how she wants to make an entrance. Dealing with garbage is her least favorite part of being a single mom. Town meetings run a close second. Some days her color-coded chore spreadsheet grows by the hour, and none of it ever really gets finished.

Amanda Willows

Amanda Willows scoops the last cookie off the baking sheet and places it in a neatly defined row.

"Only one!" Amanda warns her husband, Thomas, who's standing clear on the other side of the kitchen, nowhere near the cookies. She knows her grandmother's matcha cookies are his favorite, but she can only spare one, as these are for Cleo to hand out to the twenty-three students in her class tomorrow.

"Do you want me to stay home with Cleo during the town meeting?" Thomas asks. "I've got a few things to wrap up for work before tomorrow anyway."

Amanda's shoulders sink. She likes when they do things together, even if it is just a town meeting.

"No, it will be a good opportunity for her to watch the civic process in real time." If he's working, Cleo will be left to her own devices—baked goods taste tested and screens unmonitored.

Amanda wraps the box of cookies in foil, each fold neat and precise, the lines almost too perfect to touch. The orderly rows calm her. If the cookies are right, the rest of the evening might be, too.

"But Mom, meetings are so boring!" Cleo puts her head down on the island.

She's not wrong. Meetings are dull, but town meetings are usually a different story. They're powered almost entirely by people who like to hear their own voices, and passionate debates about things no one cared about until five minutes earlier. A familiar little spark of excitement stirs in Amanda. She loves the process of it all. The motions, the votes, the complaints, the solutions, and the possibility that something small but official might get decided.

Maybe one day, when Cleo's older, Amanda will even run for city council herself, after she's finished running every parent-teacher organization on the island. She can already picture it. Standing at the podium, sighing deeply while explaining why the new trash collection system will make the island a better place.

"Bring your book, and I'll let you play Mahjong on my phone."

Cleo fist-pumps the air. Screen time of any type is like catnip to this eight-year-old and at least Amanda can keep a watchful eye on her.

Amanda flips open her notebook and checks off cookies on her to-do list. She congratulates herself because there are only three more items on her list waiting to be completed after the meeting, assuming nothing else pops up before bedtime.

"Shoes and coat!"

Cleo takes off her house slippers and follows Amanda's request.

Amanda picks up her canvas tote from the hook by the door and smiles as Thomas gives them each a kiss on the forehead.

She glances at the clear night sky and catches a glimpse of Cassiopeia. This—a little family of her own and some purpose—is all she ever dreamt of when she was younger.

———

Calder Cunningham

Mr. Darcy, Calder Cunningham's impeccable grey British Shorthair feline, follows Calder to the foyer, where they tango as he wraps through her feet with a great big meow, imploring her to stay home. She bends and rubs his back.

"I wish I could stay," she purrs at him.

Civic duty is a necessary evil in her line of work. She must be seen to stay at the top of her realtor game. And she must ensure no one on city council makes any decisions that will impact the real estate market. So much responsibility. It's a good thing she has so much time.

Calder fastens the brass snaps on her waxed cotton field coat and pops the corduroy collar to protect her from the cold and hide any neck wrinkles her last Botox appointment missed. Mr. Darcy sits on her loafers, attempting once more to keep her home. She collects her olive-green woven leather purse that sits on the mahogany table next to her front door and taps on top of her head for her trusty readers.

Behind her, the hum of *Gilmore Girls* fills the house, the familial chatter left playing so she doesn't hear the pipes creak and the walls moan when she returns from the town meeting later tonight. The television never forgets to say goodnight.

As much as she'd prefer to stay at home with her comfort show and Mr. Darcy, Calder always thrives at a meeting—it's better than an empty house. It might be the serotonin boost she needs tonight.

The cold night air stings her face as she walks to her car. At least her cheeks will be rosy. She always looks better with a touch of color. As she starts the car, the voice of an audiobook narrator with a Scottish brogue fills the quiet space. Silence is Calder's enemy, the time that gives her mind the freedom to catastrophize or get stuck in the memories of yesteryear. Books and podcasts are the friends that erase the silence. Knitting is the vice that conquers the stillness in the house. She needs it all when her children—who would resent the term, as they're now adults—aren't at home.

Tippy Meadowcroft

Tippy Meadowcroft ignores her boyfriend, Dave Sherman, as he offers to drive her to the meeting. Instead she hops onto Bertha, her trusty bike. She always rides her bike to town meetings, even if the sky is spitting. A bit of exercise keeps her mind clear and sharp. Plus, it gives her another opportunity to gather information for her gossip column.

The ride to the meeting is seven minutes long, and in that time, she clocks Mrs. Newman in her weighted and lit vest, a delivery truck stuck in a muddy ditch, and Brandon Summers barely rolling to a stop as he leaves Thin Pines.

The church, primarily used for town business over the last few years, smells of incense and mold. The bright red carpet's stained with generations of Greensea's finest tromping in and out searching for some kind of spiritual growth. Tippy sets up her tripod in a front pew to the left of the altar, giving her a clear view of everyone who attends the meeting, and of Mayor Nickerbottom's pulpit.

"Mayor! Mayor!" Tippy calls to a man making his way to the altar, wearing a newsboy cap and carrying a folder filled with papers.

"Not now, Tippy. I've got to prepare." He takes the steps up the altar two at a time.

Tippy clasps her hands in front of her and kneels in the pew. "Tell me what this is about and I'm certain I can help you."

The mayor shushes her away with his cap. "You'll find out soon enough with the rest of Greensea."

Hmmph. Tippy's eyes narrow. Finding out before Greensea is her actual job. She begins her day at sunrise, tracking down all the news on the island. Visits all the local coffee shops. Observes the regulars boarding the ferry, waiting at the bus stop, and in line at Island Grocers. She doesn't stop until the island goes to bed. If someone gets a new car, comes into an inheritance, changes jobs, or becomes a vegan, Tippy knows before anyone else. Knowing things means she's someone. Otherwise, she's just another person sitting alone in a pew.

And somehow, tonight, she has no clue what Mayor Nickerbottom is about to say. But there's no time to play detective, as islanders file into the church.

hear ye, hear ye

Tippy Meadowcroft

(*Livestream of the Greensea Town Meeting*)
Host: Reporting live from the All-Denominational Greensea Island Church, this is Tippy Meadowcroft (*wink*), with a livestream of Greensea's Emergency Town Meeting. Let's listen to Mayor Nickerbottom.
Mayor Nickerbottom: Let the record show that this meeting is being recorded by Tippy Meadowcroft.
Host: I'm live-streaming, Mayor.
Mayor Nickerbottom: This is not a livestream pay-per-view event, Tippy. You're recording it for the people who can't make it.
Host: Tomatoes, ta-mah-toes.
Mayor Nickerbottom: Let's get down to our first, and only, order of business tonight. I called you all here because I've learned about a dire situation.
Host: (*whispers*) Look at the packed crowd of wide-eyed

islanders. For those of you not joining us in person, feel free to leave a comment.

Mayor Nickerbottom: Because of the financial struggles faced by our ferry system, they've decided to close the galley.

(*Camera falls to the floor.*)

Host: What in the world?

(*Audible hum amongst the crowd.*)

Host: (*whispers*) Greensea residents are in shock.

Woman's Voice: That has to be illegal!

Man's Voice: That doesn't make any sense! How will getting rid of the food help save money?

Calder Cunningham: Some people take the ferry for the ferry pours!

Host: (*speaks to the camera*) We know how much Calder likes her ferry pours.

(*Rolls eyes*)

Comment from GreenseaPhil123: I'll buy you a ferry wine, Calder!

Mayor Nickerbottom: Tippy! This is a meeting. We don't need a running commentary on an official town recording.

Host: (*speaks to camera—again*) Sorry!

Mayor Nickerbottom: I am aware that some of you think the ferry is the best bar in town. But keeping the galley open costs a great deal of money. There's sourcing and preparing the food. Checking everyone out. Keeping it all clean. And then to top it off, ferry workers spend an inordinate amount of time picking up after everyone.

Man's Voice: That's because no one understands the garbage system.

Mayor Nickerbottom: Yes, yes. The garbage is a bit confusing. But as you can see from this report, closing the galley will save approximately fifty thousand dollars a year.

Woman's Voice: This is a terrible idea!

Man's Voice: That's where I eat my breakfast every day.

Man's Voice: It's my coffee shop.

Woman's Voice: My lunch stop.

Mayor Nickerbottom: I understand, and that's why I've asked you all to come here today. Keep in mind, this is not my decision. I've asked the ferry people if privatizing the galley on the Greensea boat was an option. They have challenged us to see if we can come up with fifty thousand dollars to keep it running. Of course, I know my Greensea-ers, and I said game on. We will raise that money in a heartbeat.

(*Murmurs within the crowd.*)

Josh Sherman: How do you plan to raise the money?

Mayor Nickerbottom: Great question! I've put together a group of islanders who are part of different segments in the community to look at our options and come up with a plan.

Dave Sherman: Who's on the committee?

Mayor Nickerbottom: Another great question from another Sherman brother!

(*Unintelligible sound coming from the mayor.*)

Mayor Nickerbottom: As mayor of this fair isle, I nominate Laura Prescott, Amanda Willows, and Nora—I mean Calder—Cunningham.

(*Camera falls down.*)

Comment from GreenseaPhil123: A group of wonderful women. Fantastic idea, Mayor.

Tippy Meadowcroft: I nominate myself!

Mayor Nickerbottom: Tippy, you're a reporter and will observe and record.

Tippy Meadowcroft: (*Unintelligible noise.*)

Laura Prescott: Mayor, I don't know if I have time for this! I have a full-time job and I'm raising three children.

Comment from GreenseaPhil123: You're doing a bang-up job, Laura.

Calder Cunningham: Ditto! Well, not the three children part. But the time part.

Amanda Willows: And I have all my PTO responsibilities at school and a young child!

Mayor Nickerbottom: Ladies, there's nothing more important than saving our ferry as we know it, and I'm asking the three of you to work together and figure it out.

Tippy Meadowcroft: Surely you can work together for the good of our community. If not, I'm happy to take up the cause for you. Why don't you meet at Thin Pines on Wednesday at seven? You can discuss it further.

(*Camera pans to Laura, Calder, and Amanda leaning over pews to discuss.*)

Mayor Nickerbottom: Thank you, Tippy, but next time, please just observe. And with that, I call this meeting to a close.

Host: (*rolls her eyes into camera*) I think you need me more than you know, Mayor. Anywho, won't this group be one to write home about. Amanda Willows, self-proclaimed do-gooder. Laura Prescott, councilor for the island. And Calder Cunningham, the realtor who holds the keys to our dreams. Oh, Greensea, saving the ferry galley is going to be a sideshow when these three come together! Reporting live from the All-Denominational Greensea Island Church, this is Tippy Meadowcroft signing off.

———

As islanders file out of the pews and out of the church, Mayor Nickerbottom packs up his papers. Tippy packs up her tripod, while the hurt of not being chosen can't quite be packed away so easily.

"Ladies, ladies. If I could have a minute at the pulpit," asks the mayor.

Calder, Laura, Amanda, and Tippy, refusing to be ignored, walk toward the altar.

"Mayor, you know I don't have time for this," presses Laura. "My docket is full and my time is valuable."

"I can do it for you." Tippy raises her hand. The mayor mouths 'no.'

"Same! I'm too busy managing the daily chaos at the elementary school." Amanda and Laura exchange icy stares.

Tippy raises her hand again. "Me! I have time!"

"What about the other women on the island?" Laura crosses her arms.

"Like me!" Tippy pouts. She looks the three women up and down. She's not a lawyer, a realtor, or an island do-gooder, but hard work is practically her middle name.

What do they have that she doesn't?

"You can't be the gossip reporter *and* on the committee, Tippy," reprimands Amanda.

Tippy's shoulders fall and her heels dig in.

Mayor Nickerbottom turns to her. "Tippy, you are the beating pulse of this island. Your savage ability to be the one who everyone comes to with information makes you the perfect person to observe this group and share info with the rest of the island." The mayor rubs his beard as a small twinkle returns to Tippy's eyes after the compliment.

"Mayor, I'd like to ask you why you haven't asked any men on the island to be on this committee?" asks Calder.

Laura examines the group. "Yeah! Good point!" She nods as if she's ready to high-five Calder and continues. "I'd hope that it wasn't a sexist oversight, but I fear that it's an attempt to continue to have women carry the unseen heavy load of work behind the scenes." She puts her hands on her hips in her best courtroom stance.

Tippy wonders if she should have Laura on retainer—just in case.

Mayor Nickerbottom's mouth drops open. "Of course not." He stares at the ceiling. He must be hoping for divine intervention. "I picked all of you because you're the movers and shakers on the island. You get things done. Do you think I could leave this in the hands of the Sherman brothers?"

"Hey!" says Tippy, ready to defend her boyfriend and his brothers. "You know they are wildly capable men...in everything they do." She giggles despite herself.

"Spare us," says Calder, rolling her eyes.

"You know what I mean." Mayor Nickerbottom scratches his head. "Laura, somehow you manage all the island's legal issues and hold down a house with three growing children." The corners of Laura's mouth creep up. The mayor wipes his brow.

"Calder, you have raised two of the island's shining stars while being the top realtor on the island and in the Seattle area. You've created an empire and a name for yourself."

Calder raises her chin while Mayor Nickerbottom sticks his hands in his pockets.

"Amanda, every single day you make Greensea Elementary better and better. For heaven's sake—when I heard the lengths you went to to create a homegrown lunch program for those kids, I almost called the Alice Waters Association."

Amanda's smile holds a beat longer than necessary.

Mayor Nickerbottom lets out a sigh and returns to the discussion. "The men? Sure, they are all capable, but they can't multi-task and create something out of nothing like you all can." He runs his hands through his hair. "This is not a punishment. This is because I see you as the most capable people on the island. It's a coincidence that you identify as women. Although I do suspect it is the reason you are so accomplished."

The women exchange glances.

"But you need a fourth! Even Mount Rushmore has four!" Tippy launches one last attempt.

Mayor Nickerbottom's eyebrows twist. "This is a committee, not a national monument. Three for voting purposes, Tippy."

She almost catches her hair in her jacket as she zips it in anger.

"Thin Pines Wednesday at seven?" Mayor Nickerbottom raises his lip, waiting for an answer.

"I need to check my showings," answers Calder.

"And I'll need to check my kids' schedules," replies Laura.

Mayor Nickerbottom looks to Amanda. "I'll make sure Thomas will be home, but I'm pretty certain it won't be a problem for me."

Amanda turns on her heel to leave.

"Give her a clipboard and a cause, and she's all in," remarks Tippy.

Amanda turns. "Why do you make it sound like a flaw?"

Amanda's cheeks flush, and Tippy swears she notices her eyes tear up as she makes her way out of the church. She shouldn't have directed her anger toward Amanda. This isn't her fault.

———

Tippy can't decide whether the cool February air on her cheeks or Mayor Nickerbottom's dismissal stings more as she straps on her helmet over her long auburn hair. She swings a leg over Bertha and pedals onto the dark street, her bike light shining a narrow path ahead.

"Why didn't he name me to the committee?" she mutters, pedaling almost as fast as her thoughts are spinning. Surely he knows she can do both—record and participate. Tippy is the queen of multi-hyphenate living. She won't be sidelined.

"Aargh!" she screams into the sea-soaked air.

Her unexpected voice startles an owl, who hoots in the distance. The tall pine trees frame the street. Bertha's motor kicks in as Tippy climbs the hill. Her feet, powered by her anger, are moving so fast that she doesn't even notice Dave pull up next to her in his truck.

"What's got you in a tizzy?" he asks, leaning out of the window as his truck creeps along.

"No one puts Tippy Meadowcroft in the corner!" The owl hoots again, and Dave rolls to a stop.

"Get in, Red," Dave says as Tippy continues to pedal.

She huffs as she continues up the hill.

"Let me pop Bertha in the back and drive you home. It's dark and you're a danger to small island animals jutting out into your path with so much pent-up anger."

Tippy brakes. And hops off the bike. Dave throws the truck in park, gets out, and picks up Bertha.

"Be careful with her!" Bertha is one of Tippy's favorite possessions, next to her toy poodle.

"Bear, Bertha, Dave. I know the order of things around here." Dave winks as Tippy pushes by him to the passenger side of the truck.

Dave climbs into the driver's seat. "Still mad ol' Nickerbottom didn't pick you to be on the committee?"

Tippy slumps back in her seat. "It smarts."

"Babe, everyone has to have a chance to shine. It can't all be the Tippy show."

The Tippy Show. Now there's an idea. Tippy listens to the soft country song crooning on the radio.

"Do you think it's because I'm not a mom?" she asks Dave.

"You think Mayor Nickerbottom only asked people with kids to save the galley that everyone uses?" Dave turns to look at her.

"No, but it's the only thing they have that I don't!" She twirls a long piece of hair around her index finger.

"I think it's about all the things you have and do, not what you lack."

Tippy rubs her temples. Dave is always more sensible, and it's annoying.

"By the end of this, the mayor and all of Greensea will see who the real boss is and always has been."

Dave nods his head with a chuckle.

They pull up to Meadowcroft—Tippy's family's property. Her mom's farmstand sits waiting for the spring daffodils. Her parents live down the hill while Tippy and Dave live in her grandmother's old home, surrounded by several acres of gardens. It's usually idyllic, even in the dark. But tonight, with the breeze rustling through the leaves, Tippy finds anything but peace here.

Like a balloon that's lost all its air, Tippy trudges into the house, kicks off her shoes, and scoops up Bear. The brown, fuzzy creature kisses her on the cheek as she storms to her overstuffed couch and plops down.

"Mama's good little boy," she coos.

She rearranges the pillows behind her back and sets her feet on the coffee table in front of her. Tippy gives her nails a once-over and chews on her index finger—a habit that began in middle school and only appears now when she's mad. To distract herself, she re-watches the video she recorded of the town meeting.

Amazed at her own videography skills, she mentally pats herself on the back for catching Laura, Calder, and Amanda's reactions to being nominated. Laura, wide eyed with a furrowed brow, waiting to pounce on the opposing counsel—in this case, Mayor Nickerbottom. Calder, all perfectly coifed chestnut-brown chignon, with the only hint of annoyance sitting on her open, rose-painted lips. And Amanda, black hair in a sleek pony, an oversized fluffy scarf attempting to swallow her whole, barely exposing her flushed cheeks and her bottom lip tucked under her upper canines. Amanda's daughter sits next to her, balling her fists like her mom won a prize.

The three women pop on the screen. Tippy watches it all

again. Whatever she's watching is something. It is compelling TV.

The gears slowly shift into place. There's got to be a new role for her here—something she can do—whether Mayor Nickerbottom wants her to or not.

Dave cracks open a beer in the kitchen and Bear settles into the crook of her arm.

And then, while she strokes Bear's head and Dave takes a long sip of the Greensea IPA, the metaphorical clouds part and a sunbeam illuminates something in Tippy's head.

"Jackpot!" Bear jumps off Tippy's lap with a yelp.

Dave sets the beer on the butcher block counter in the kitchen. "Figure out all the world's problems?"

Tippy raises her hand like an explorer discovering a new land. "Yes! The Save the Ferry committee is sure to garner attention, so in turn recording the meetings will be more popular than the regular town meetings."

"And I know you love nothing more than turning nothing into something!" Dave strolls over to the overstuffed couch and kisses Tippy on the head. "You're not still on your quest to film a reality TV show on Greensea, are you?"

Dave knows her too well.

Ever since Tippy watched Greensea grab the spotlight with the secret arrival of Johnny Nickel—the world's biggest popstar —she's sought to capitalize and expand on that bit of internet fame. With the excitement of Johnny and island darling Jac Sherman's wedding behind them, people must be clamoring for more Greensea in their lives. After the producers of the popular dating show *Love at the Last Resort* rejected Tippy's bid to use Greensea Island as the setting for their show, Tippy Meadowcroft became even more steadfast in her dream of creating a reality TV show on Greensea Island. Could this be the right platform to watch all her ideas flourish? Maybe, but she has to start small and build some small momentum.

She makes a mental list of all the things she'll need to do to edit the meetings and turn them into a compelling viral video. Of course, all the extra attention will only amplify the cause and make the job of the committee that much easier.

"I'm helping everyone," Tippy says to herself.

She grabs her laptop. Searches the web for a template for a video release form. Finds one and sends it over to Laura, Calder, and Amanda.

If Mayor Nickerbottom and the producers at that stupid TV network are going to ignore her and all her good ideas— she'll show them what they are all missing and that she doesn't need them anyway.

the early wedgie gets the worm

Laura Prescott

The clock says 7:16 a.m., the sun's barely above the horizon, Laura Prescott's high-rise pants are giving her a wedgie, and the burnt toast is getting cold. She's shouted upstairs seven times to get her offspring out of bed.

Laura wonders if it's too early to wish the day away.

Mayor Nickerbottom's speech last night had her on a high, but this morning she can't even accomplish the simplest tasks. The usual parenting pep talks run through her mind—find the joy, the days are long but the years are short—but it's the lure of her overpriced Troll House latte that pushes her forward. She knows there's no other way out than through it. It's time to get these kids on their merry way.

"Jo, Meg, George! Let's go!" she screams one more time before returning to the kitchen.

Somewhere along the line, Laura decided her "thing" would be packing lunches full of love notes, each fruit and veggie cut into social media-worthy shapes. Today she's slicing an apple, cutting a heart from the center, and plugging it with a matching piece of melon, hoping some kid will go home bragging about what a great mom the Prescott kids have. Maybe then she'll finally be forgiven for the nacho cheese chip snack of 2020.

The butcher block counter looks like the scene of a fruit salad massacre. Single parent guilt combined with her desire to look like she has it all together equals a mess she can barely control today. But the kitchen will have to wait until she returns from work.

Daughter one, Jo, and daughter two, Meg, make their appearance at 7:32—four minutes later than usual. Meg packs her bag and grabs her toast to eat in the car on the way to school. Jo drops the bread in the garbage and opens the pantry and snags a handful of Oreos instead. A tiny part of Laura hopes the crumbs get stuck in between her teeth.

"You can't still be mad that I won't let my eighteen-year-old daughter be on a dating app." Laura had been searching for Phil on Buoy—the local dating site—when she found Jo on there.

"I'm eighteen!" Jo looks at her with a sneer reserved only for the person who brought you into this world.

"And you live in...." Laura starts.

"Your house, eat your food, and I am not financially independent." Jo completes her sentence. "I know that, but it doesn't mean you should control every part of my life."

"Thanks, Ma," says Meg, kissing her on the cheek, ignoring the argument taking place around her.

Part of Laura's heart cracks open as she watches them walk to the car. Ever since they were preschoolers, she wouldn't let them go to school upset. But now, during these teenage years while she's a single parent, she can't help it. The family balance is thrown off, and she's always on the wrong side of the tightrope, dangling over a pit of angry teenagers with expensively straight teeth.

But they're off to school and now it's just son number one, child number three—George.

"Ready?" she asks, taking note that he's fully dressed and has two matching shoes on. Win one for the day.

"Yeppers, Mama-roni!" He bounds over to Laura with his arms up. She gives him a quick smell check. Score one for the soap and another one for George for using it.

"What's with the hair?" His black hair is parted down the side and slicked back with some substance that seems to have left a residue.

"It's Dress Like Your Role Model Day and I'm dressed like the kid from Home Alone."

Of course he is, and she doesn't even care that he should have a better role model, because he took it upon himself to remember what day it was. A jolt of pride rips through her body. She's convinced the school's mission is to keep moms on their toes—or drive them mad—by inventing dress-up days destined to go in one ear and out the other.

"Grab your stuff and hop into Betty White. I'll be right there." Laura can taste the victory—coffee is so close.

Gathering her papers from the counter, she tosses them in her satchel and heads out to the overpriced car Phil gave her before he told her he didn't love her anymore. As if a hunk of metal would make up for walking out on their twenty-year marriage. China…it was supposed to be china symbolizing their durability. Instead, he acted like the bull and shattered it all. Laura shakes away her anger like a duck shaking water off its back.

Back to the reality in front of her.

"Remember, George, Blake's mom is taking you to and from soccer practice today."

"Got it." He gives her a double thumbs up. "But do I have to do the warm-ups she makes Blake do?"

"Nope." She shakes her head. Blake is eight going on full

college scholarship athlete. Maybe to the detriment of her kids, Laura has never subscribed to the child prodigy narrative. They don't even have a family shelf filled with trophies.

She tosses her stuff on the passenger seat, and George climbs into the backseat. Greensea Elementary is only a four-minute drive from the house, and if she times it correctly, she won't have to wait too long in the drop-off line. Which is exactly what she's accomplished today. Running their mornings with military precision helps quell some of the chaos in Laura's mind.

She barely pulls to a complete stop in front of the school before Georgie opens the door and hops out.

"Family rules, Georgie?" she yells, knowing they're ingrained in his brain.

"Listen to adults and don't be a d*&k!"

The door closes before she can remind him that's not exactly their family rule. But kid number three has a more mature vocabulary than she planned on. As if on cue, PTO president—and mom of the year, according to George—Amanda Willows drives by with her jaw on the ground. Nothing in Laura's life can happen without an audience. Living on Greensea Island is akin to living in a fishbowl.

Betty White's almost on autopilot driving away from the shame and toward the coffee she desperately needs before she goes to the office to mediate island residents' squabbles—which are as annoying as her teenage daughters bickering.

She pulls up to Troll House Coffee, with a rounded brown door made of slabs of wood, a green sloped roof, and a water wheel on the side. Objectively the cutest coffee spot in the state of Washington, maybe the world. The drive-through window is even dressed in a green-and-white gingham curtain.

The curtain opens and a little lady with short salt-and-pepper hair peers out. "What can I get ya?" Vera asks.

Laura is always surprised she doesn't recognize the car—or

her order, but maybe Vera doesn't pay much attention. Even though Laura is here every day, like clockwork.

"I'll have a triple caff vanilla latte with oat milk, please."

"Sorry, sweets. No goat's milk anymore." Vera pushes up her glasses and taps her pen on the pad of paper she uses to take down the orders.

"Oh, no, I said oat milk." Maybe Vera's hearing is going with her memory.

"Don't carry that. How 'bout some almond milk?"

"I've been ordering the same thing here every morning for ages, and nobody has ever said anything about not having oat milk."

"That's because I thought you were ordering goat's milk and we had it until yesterday when the mayor, who sticks his nose in everyone's business, found out and made us throw it out. Apparently, it's not legal"—Vera uses air quotes—"to sell unpasteurized goat's milk."

Laura gulps. She's been drinking raw goat's milk all this time. Her stomach twists. Gross. She hopes she's been vaccinated against farm animal viruses. She vomits in her mouth.

"I think I'll skip my drink today."

Vera shrugs, and Laura rolls up the window and pulls away. Apollo Bakeshop will have to do.

Her phone pings as she drives. On a normal day, she'd be at her desk right now, and she's sure her assistant, Becky, is wondering where she is.

Weaving around the car line for the ferry, Laura drives down Main Street and pulls into a parking spot in front of the bakery. Across the street, Tippy Meadowcroft leads a gaggle of Fit Greenies—seniors on Greensea—down the sidewalk in a series of high knees and lunges. Laura can't help but wonder if that's her future: sidestepping down Main Street with her Pilates peers once they retire from the reformer.

"Check your email," Tippy yells from across the street. "You need to sign something before our meeting."

After mentally adding Tippy's to-do to her long list, the sweet smell of cinnamon rolls draws her attention toward her new destination. If only she had time to sit and devour one of the freshly made concoctions. But, no, she must take a deposition from Cooper Winksalot regarding his wayward donkey.

As she stands in line at the bakeshop catching up on her emails, she notices Tippy's request for the members of the committee to sign a video and photo release. She rolls her eyes. She'll get to it later. An icon with a name next to it pops up on her screen. She can't quite read it without her readers. Jeez. There's no end to the way scammers will try to get a hold of you nowadays. She swipes it away without giving it another thought.

"May I take your order?" asks the woman behind the counter.

"Um, yes. Sorry. Just a sec. Do you have o-a-t milk?" Laura will not risk another milk mix up.

The woman squints her eyes. "Yes, we have oat milk." She enunciates the single syllable.

"Thank goodness. May I have a triple-caff vanilla latte with oat milk?"

The woman nods, writes Laura's order on the cup, and rings it up.

Laura's phone rings again as she sits on a stool at the window bar. She holds the screen a foot from her face.

Greensea Elementary.

Shit.

"Mrs. Prescott?" says a female voice on the other end.

"Ms. Prescott," she corrects her. She can't fathom why it matters to her now, but her compulsion to correct people is overwhelming.

"I'm sorry, ma'am. Principal Atkins asked me to call you."

Laura can't focus on the words coming through the phone.

She scoots the device away from her and puts her head down on the counter and curses the underwear that kicked off this fiasco of a morning. All she can do is wish for some magic ferry dust to rewind time and make this morning disappear.

"O-a-t milk latte for Laura," the barista calls out.

Laura snatches the coffee without placing a lid on top, letting it dribble down her grey turtleneck as she hightails it out the door.

clothes make the (wo)man

Amanda Willows

Amanda Willows runs into the house to change out of her school drop-off uniform—turtleneck, wool coat, gnome print pajama pants, and slippers. The outfit hides her pjs from anyone she drives by and leaves them thinking she's ready for the day.

From the outside, she passes. That's enough for now.

Plus, skipping a full getting-ready routine buys her a few sacred minutes to scroll Instagram—just enough time to clock who's already crushed a sunrise workout in a mirrored home gym, shared a "get ready with me" from a gleaming marble bathroom, and posted a breezy "how lucky am I" selfie from an early morning ferry—before she makes Cleo organic old-fashioned oats with sliced fruit and braids her hair in whatever style Cleo declares the winner that day—fishtail, French, waterfall, bubble. It's anyone's guess each morning, but it's always elaborate and sometimes requires a tutorial. Regardless, they are precious moments she gets to spend with her only child, who's growing up too quickly.

Amanda walks over to the windowsill and grabs a mason jar,

then moves to the cabinet and takes out her flour. Time to feed the sourdough, her first job after successfully getting Cleo off for the day. She bakes her loaves on Sundays, letting the smell rise through the house. It signals a return to the work week and the end of the weekend.

"What's your plan for the day?" Thomas asks as he puts his coffee cup in the sink.

"It's Role Model Day! I'm going to hand out the snack to each of the classrooms. Then I'll run to Island Grocers before I go back to pick up Cleo for dance. And if I have time, I might do some prep for our Save the Ferry committee meeting." Amanda leaves out any mention of the reality TV she plans to watch during the day. It's her stress relief, her way of focusing on something other than her own life. Everyone has something. Some moms pour a glass of wine, but Amanda presses play.

Thomas reaches for his brown leather messenger bag, hanging on the hook next to the side door.

"Cleo's eight now. You know you're not getting paid to volunteer. There are other parents who can pitch in and help. Maybe it's time to start picking up some shifts at the clinic," Thomas says as he peeks in his bag that Amanda packed for him.

Even the thought of going back to the clinic gives her indigestion.

"Thomas, you know how important it is to be available during the tween years. They are pivotal to a child's development." She will go back to work sometime. Truly, she will. But Cleo is her priority right now. What if Cleo is bullied at school and doesn't have anyone to come home to? Amanda was a latchkey kid and will not let the same fate befall her daughter.

"I'm not suggesting you take an international assignment for months on end. Just sub at the clinic. The extra cash would really help. Plus, things don't have to be perfect around here." He glides his hand around the kitchen. "A frozen dinner once in a while won't do any harm."

That sounds like a slippery slope to Amanda. Frozen meatballs today, Salisbury steak TV dinners tomorrow. She prides herself on preservative free cooking. Thomas's requests will not waylay her parenting principles.

"Let me get a handle on how much time the ferry committee will take and then I'll look. Promise."

She knows that next to Cleo and herself, the ferry galley is one of the most important things to Thomas, as he consumes at least one meal a day on the boat. She hopes the threat of it disappearing is enough to quell his complaints about her time spent on that.

"I'm sure you could do a day at the clinic while you figure that out." He kisses the top of her forehead. Thomas turns on his heel and leaves for the ferry.

Amanda lets out a sigh as the side door closes. The clinic used to be her happy place, with the clean smell of antiseptic and the routine of taking vitals. But the thought of having anyone else watching Cleo, even for a few hours after school, fills her with dread. Instead, she finds ways to keep herself busy that revolve around Cleo. And obviously the opportunities mostly revolve around Greensea Elementary. Wisely, she didn't tell Thomas that the other day, the mailman tracked her down at school with a package that needed a signature.

It doesn't help that she's seen the volunteer work of the other parents. Someone sent in an empty tampon box for the Celebration of Platonic Friendships—a.k.a. Valentine's Day, but they're not allowed to say that. That fiasco required an impromptu lesson on feminine hygiene, leaving seven-year-old Jeannie Frank waking up at 2 a.m. convinced she was about to bleed to death.

Luckily, as the leader of the Greensea Girl Scout troop, Amanda had access to enough recycled cookie boxes to save the day. There's no question she's the most qualified parent to take charge at Greensea Elementary and no matter how much

Thomas complains, she has to be there today. Without her, things fall apart. They're counting on her.

Cleo wore her great-grandmother's kimono to school today, and Amanda needs to change into her Amelia Earhart outfit. An easy costume that won't get in the way while she hands out the fruit leathers at snack time.

At least she's allowed herself some time to catch up on her reality TV du jour while she gets ready. *Housewives* on Monday and Wednesday. *Below Deck* on Tuesday. *Selling Sunset* or *Buying Beverly Hills* on Thursday or Friday. Thirty-eight minutes of guilty pleasure where she can break the household screen rules and not have to think about anything. Yes, life would be easier if she didn't have such strict rules about acceptable television. She's inadvertently sucked all the joy out of the stupid screen.

After she's successfully deduced that the hot Australian bosun is about to be fired on *Below Deck*, she's free to save the day at school.

As Amanda pulls into her parking spot, Laura Prescott marches out of the front door of the school, her feet moving a mile a minute.

Amanda throws the car in park and gets out. "I'm glad I saw you," Amanda says. "Is that form Tippy sent over aboveboard? Should I be worried about anything?"

"I only skimmed it. I'll check it out when I get back to the office and let you know if I have any concerns."

Laura moves a tube of something around in her hands. Her fingers don't quite cover the lettering.

"KY Jelly?" Amanda's eyebrows rise.

She tries to stick it in the pocket of her blazer but the words "personal lubricant" stick out.

"You're walking out of an elementary school with KY jelly?" Did George bring it in for show and tell? Amanda racks her brain, wondering if there are other uses for the lubricant that will save her from having to explain its intended use. Reason number 76 she needs to be at school as much as possible to prevent these things from happening.

Laura's face turns crimson.

"Calm down, Amanda. We can't all be as perfect as you and Cleo."

Perfect? If she only knew Amanda was wearing her underwear inside out because there wasn't any clean laundry.

Laura bends the tube into her pocket. "It's not a big deal. Georgie thought it was hair gel. Just picking it up so it doesn't cause any more trouble in the classroom." She finally throws it in her purse. "Georgie found it in the back of a cabinet. It's probably expired."

Expired sex gel...even better.

"At least it wasn't a box of condoms?" Amanda shrugs, eliciting a huff from Laura. Amanda's jokes never land the way she intends. "I'll see you tonight at our meeting."

Laura nods her head. "I'm late. I have to get to work."

The PTO president bristles as she emphasizes the word *work*.

"As do I!" Amanda chirps with a smile and lifts the box of organic fruit leathers she procured from Fork & Stable.

Laura opens her car door and looks up before she climbs in. "Oh, that's great! Are you finally on the payroll here?" She doesn't wait for a response. Her white not-a-mom-van purrs as she backs out of the parking spot.

It's barely 9 a.m. and this is the second mention Amanda Willows has had about her lack of employment. She gets it—in order to count, you have to have a job. Ugh. What she would do to go home and watch an episode of *Real Housewives of Anywhere*. At least their drama would make her stop thinking about her own life.

Her stomach gurgles as she swallows a burp. She sets the box down on the sidewalk and straightens the flight goggles threatening to strangle her.

"Morning, Amanda!" Patricia buzzes her in the front door of the school and scoops her badge out of the drawer of the desk.

"Who are you dressed as, Patricia?" She's wearing an oversized grey knit poncho over a black shirt.

"Martha Stewart!"

Yikes! That's what she wore when she left prison. Sex gels, inmates... Amanda can't imagine what would happen if she weren't here to run interference. She needs to get into the classroom. The fate of the future is in her hands.

"I'm going to hand out the treats," she says, and escapes to the hallway.

A smile forms on her lips as the smell of glue and tempera paint wafts through the corridors. Little voices bellow out of classrooms. Kids barely taller than her knees push past her as she walks to the first room. This is where Amanda is most comfortable.

"Hi, Mrs. Harris!" She hands her the pre-counted and labeled bundle for her class.

"Thank you, dear! Sure hope these taste more like fruit than leather." She takes them to her desk.

So does Amanda. Ash and Vic Willard at Fork & Stable worked so hard to create them. Pureeing, cooking, and then dehydrating their apples so Greensea Elementary could have enough for every child. Everyone wants this to be a win. The PTO spent a disproportionate amount of their budget on this new snack creation, but it was the only way to ensure there wouldn't be any complaints, and they could meet all the dietary and allergen restrictions. Amanda can't wait until the next school newsletter says, *Amanda Willows has saved snack time.* Then Thomas will realize she's doing something worthwhile, even without adding to their 401k.

Her stomach grumbles—again. She grabs one of the extra

treats and takes a bite. It's chewy and sticky. She's worried the crown may pop off of her molar. Shit, she hopes no one loses a tooth today! That would put a damper on all the accolades she's hoping for.

Behind her, a little voice declares fruit isn't a treat. Someone else asks if it's a dog treat or a people treat.

Shiitake mushrooms.

This pricey idea isn't a grand slam.

Stifling a multitude of burps, she hands out the fruit leathers to each classroom. What's wrong with her stomach? Amanda wonders. She throws the box down in the hallway and runs into the miniature bathroom. It's one of the ones with the toilet six inches off the ground so the little kids can reach it. She drops to the floor, twists the goggles to the back of her neck, and holds her head over the kiddie-sized bowl and throws up.

Did she spontaneously throw up from the fruit? Oh no! What if all the kids get sick too? She gags again. No, it can't be that. If it were the fruit, there'd be a bunch of munchkins already getting sick in here with her. Must be something else. Come to think of it, Amanda's stomach's been off since Thomas lodged his complaints this morning. It's all the stress he's decided to throw on her plate.

She stumbles out of the stall to find Patricia washing her hands at a miniature sink. She didn't realize anyone else was in there. She works so hard to curate her image, and it doesn't include being sick.

Their eyes meet in the mirror, and Patricia raises her eyebrows. "You feeling okay, Mrs. Willows? A little too much to drink at Wine Down last night after the town meeting?" she asks.

"Certainly not! You know I don't go there!" Amanda doesn't get invited to things like that, and she's not brave enough to go without an invitation. She unzips her leather flight jacket and fans herself with a paper towel. "I must have a bug."

"Well, then you shouldn't be around the children. Go on home and get some rest."

With that, Amanda makes a beeline for the front door of the school and hops in her minivan to return home. She races through her monumental to-do list, wondering what she can chuck without Thomas noticing so she can have a few minutes to lie down and knock whatever it is out of her system. She'll pick up a frozen lasagna from Island Grocers, throw away the box—Thomas can't win—and call it dinner.

match this

Calder Cunningham

Calder Cunningham mindlessly swipes right, right, right through potential matches on the dating app while her office assistant slides a batch of chocolate chip cookies into the oven at her newest listing. The smell always lingers, welcoming prospective buyers. She swipes again at her phone, and her foot catches on a handwoven wool rug when she stumbles over a profile for Laura Prescott. Calder braces herself on a leather armchair.

"You okay, Ms. Cunningham?" asks her assistant.

Calder clears her throat. "Yes, yes. Just turning on all the lights." She reaches for the lamp on the end table next to the chair.

Well, well, well...

What an entrance to the dating world! There's a picture of Laura sitting on the beach laughing. She's radiant. Even youthful. A fresh face in a stale dating app. And she's competition. There are so few eligible men in her suitable age range, and Laura is a catch any way you look at it. Well educated. Fit. Naturally blonde.

Calder inhales, wishing she were by herself. She's well versed at putting on a poker face, but sometimes she doesn't have the energy. And now she must go about her showing and pretend she's not worried about the fresh threat to her quest for happiness.

She straightens the waist of her pristine ivory slacks and paints on her happy facade.

> Calder: You finally took the next step! Happy to see you on the app!

A little white lie never hurt anyone.

> Laura: Ugh. It's not me. It's the "in" thing for eighteen-year-olds to do. Thanks for letting me know Jo's profile is still up there.

Hmmm. There's no mistaking it's Laura in the picture. Honestly, Calder might be tempted to pretend she didn't post it, too, with that bio. Frisky Cat Herder? What was Laura thinking? The photo works but not the rest.

> Calder: Well, then you must have a twin.

Three dots appear and then disappear.

Calder peers in the foyer mirror. No lipstick on her teeth? Check. Brown hair smooth and in place? Check. Check. Thoughts about an island peer tucked behind her perfectly hued cheeks? Check. Telltale signs of her age masked by expensive lotions. Without a doubt. Satisfied, she swings open the front door for the buyers who requested a showing of this multi-million-dollar property, the warm scent of cookies drifting through the foyer.

Carefully placed solar lanterns line the driveway, creating a gentle, not-so-dark glow. Inside, the gas fireplaces are roaring, and soft piano music floats through the built-in speakers. This is far from Calder's first rodeo—she wants the Andersons' shoulders to relax as if they've stepped into a peaceful sanctuary after a long day at work.

Every detail has been curated. The throw blanket artfully rumpled on the armchair, the fresh hydrangeas on the dining table, the faint citrus-clean scent that whispers "effortless."

Mr. Anderson walks in first—not a ladies-first kind of man —and his eyes go straight to the ceiling. "No security system, I see?"

Calder laughs. "Not necessary on Greensea Island." Greensea's crime rate is the lowest in the state and quite possibly the entire West Coast. It's an island; the worst crime they've had is when someone stole Mrs. Rasputin's pie off of her windowsill. And to be honest, everyone's pretty sure it was Mr. Harrow's horse.

"It's always necessary." Mr. Anderson steps further into the house. "Hardwired for Internet?"

"Very few homes are hardwired, but I think you'll find some of the best connectivity in this part of the island." Calder follows close behind.

"I need my home to be hardwired."

"In tech?" she asks, knowing the answer, because of course she Googled her prospective buyer.

Mr. Anderson nods.

"I'll put you in touch with, ummm...the CIO of Intellitech." Stupid perimenopause. Things, especially names, are no longer at the tip of her tongue.

"Ravi?" Mr. Anderson asks.

"Yes." How could she forget his name? "He'll let you know what he's done to his home."

Mr. Anderson stops in his tracks, turns, and looks at Calder. "He lives on Greensea?"

She nods. "Yes, I sold him his home about five years ago."

Score one for Calder. She can already see the gears turning behind his eyes—the checklist of must-haves, the imagined missing items, the looming possibility of a lowball offer disguised as a "concern." Tech bros are predictable if nothing else.

"It smells divine in here," Mrs. Anderson says as they move into the kitchen.

"Let me get the cookies out of the oven." Calder walks over to the stainless steel eight-burner range.

"A Wolf?" squeals Mrs. Anderson.

Bingo.

"Only the best appliances in this abode!" Calder radiates calm and confidence.

Mrs. Anderson moves in close to Calder like she's about to tell her a secret. "To be honest, I had no idea what we'd find on this island!"

Calder doesn't even need to glance at her; the tone alone tells her the woman is already imagining holiday dinners and Instagram stories captioned "weekend home."

"I've got you covered. Would you like me to show you around or do you want to take a look on your own?"

Mr. Anderson's halfway up the front staircase.

"I've got it," he replies.

He seems like a do-it-on-his-own kind of guy, so Calder stands over the sink nibbling on a cookie while she waits for them to return. She exhales, letting the warmth of the dough melt on her tongue. Selling houses is easy. Selling the idea of a life—peace, stability, space to breathe—that is the real art.

"This is the most expensive house on the market right now?" Mr. Anderson asks as he makes his way back into the kitchen.

"Yes, it is."

"Good. Good."

A buyer who only wants the most expensive object and doesn't care about anything else. Greensea won't be their primary residence. They'll jet back and forth between Seattle and San Francisco as every other proper tech bro does.

Greensea is an island of the haves and the haves-more. Calder has perfected the mask she wears around each potential buyer—first time homeowner to multi-million-dollar second home. She can handle them all.

Mr. Anderson pops a cookie into his mouth, wipes his hands together—scattering crumbs on the floor—and says, "I'll be in touch."

Mrs. Anderson crinkles her nose and squeezes Calder's arm. "I can't wait to use that bathtub," she whispers before they leave.

Cha-ching. Another notch in Calder's belt.

She texts the homeowner to let them know the showing went well, locks the house up, and climbs into her Land Rover. Just as her audiobook and the voice of the lovely Scotsman is luring his lady back to his lair, Calder's phone rings.

"Hey, Mom!" Fitz's voice is a balm for her soul, even beating out the sexy Scot. It always makes something unclench in her chest. With the kids gone, her house echoes and whole hours go unclaimed.

"Hi, sweetie! How are you?"

"Good! Good!"

She hears the wind whirling around him as he walks around campus. Calls to Mom are harder in a dorm room filled with roommates, but boy, does it fill her heart that he takes a walk and calls her every night.

"How are you? What are you up to?"

Her kind boy. He's better than his sister, Fern, about checking in on Calder. "I'm leaving a showing."

"Nice. Nice."

"Heading home to Mr. Darcy."

"Give him a back scratch for me."

"He'll be happy to see you over spring break; we all will."

She's careful not to ask too many questions. He's easier, but his sister's harder. One question, fine. Two, and the answers are shorter. Three, and they're practically ready to hang up. Sometimes texting works better. Being a mom to college kids is like walking along the edge of a cliff. You're never sure which step is going to send you right into a ravine. Gone are the days when they needed you for sustenance and basic life necessities. Now you must make them want to choose to talk to you, to come home, spend time with you. For the most part, it's not an issue. But when Darden throws a flashy vacation on a yacht in the Caribbean in their laps, of course they'll choose that over hanging out on Greensea with Mom.

"Love you, Mom." Fitz hangs up as Calder pulls into the driveway.

She slips on her house slippers and hangs up her tote. Mr. Darcy's purr echoes above the din of the TV.

Will she ever get used to the quiet? It's been months since Fitz left for college and two years since Fern left, but she still misses tripping over the shoes in the foyer, the dirty dishes in the sink, and the missing spoons. The hole in her heart is still there regardless of what she portrays on the exterior. She can't seem to fill it, no matter how much she attempts to fill it with work. She's like a house with a gorgeous stone facade and all the curb appeal with black mold hidden in its crevices. Sometimes she wonders if things would be less lonely if she'd continued to turn a blind eye to Darden's escapades. She was losing her soul, but at least she had someone to take out the garbage and another human making noise in her too-big home.

Calder pads to the kitchen and scrambles herself an egg, adding cottage cheese to ensure she gets the extra protein people say women of her age need. Aging is exhausting. She knows it's a privilege, but between the protein, the hormones, the ever-growing list of supplements—ashwagandha, magnesium, a multi-vitamin, and beetroot—it's a full-time job. And does it do anything anyway? Some days she's Wonder Woman, but others she's held together with serums and self-help podcasts.

Tonight, scrambling eggs in a quiet kitchen, she feels every one of her years settling into her bones. Or maybe it's just the new competition on the dating app, Buoy, that's adding to her malaise.

take the wheel

Laura Prescott

Laura sits paralyzed in Betty White in the driveway in front of her immaculate white colonial with green shutters and a manicured front lawn. Her hands grip the steering wheel while the heavy scent of the rotisserie chicken she picked up for dinner fills the car. She swipes on the notifications on her phone again as they pop up at a speed known only to Olympians.

Tommy Johnson.

Bradford Winston.

Gavin Tomlinson.

What. In. The. Actual...

Bailiff, seize control of her life. Calder was right. Someone has violated all her privacy and posted a dating profile without her permission.

Laura closes her eyes and braces herself. Three more notifications with random names pop up. She swipes on the most recent and it takes her to a message from Herb Rutherford—International banker looking to invest in you —that says: I'll wrangle your pussy cats anytime you need help. She throws the phone on the opposite seat. Gross! She's a well-respected attorney. How dare he sexualize her like that!

Deep breaths. She has to see what has prompted someone to say that to her. She picks her phone back up and clicks on Buoy and looks at the profile.

```
Laura Prescott—Frisky cat herder looking for
a good time.
```

So many emotions course through her. Her eyeballs might pop out of their sockets, or she might combust right here in Betty White. This small-town lawyer will be the joke of the courtroom.

The dating profile has a picture of Laura sitting on an enormous piece of driftwood at golden hour. She remembers that moment. They were all on the beach together laughing at something George was saying. Her hair's swinging in the breeze. It's a good picture, and she'd post it anywhere, but she doesn't want it on a dating app.

She turns her phone over, like if she can't see the screen, her profile will disappear.

Who posted this? An opponent in the courtroom? Surely Old Man Johnson wouldn't have done it. She lost his case, but there was not a chance in hell the ferry system was going to let his horse and buggy on the ferry. Her only other nemesis is Phil, but he would never do this to her.

She leans her head back on the seat. Not many people have access to that picture—to be exact, only the kids and Laura have that picture on their camera rolls. And those words...she's compared parenting to cat herding.

Shit. It's all so clear now.

Obviously, someone cares more about her words than her burnt toast. But putting her on a dating app is a bold move. Jo knows how Laura feels about privacy. This is a blatant violation. How could Jo do this to her?

Laura unbuckles her seatbelt, storms toward the house, and throws open the front door.

She calls up to Jo at the top of her lungs. No one would know what was going on inside if they looked at the neat exterior of the house.

"Mama-roni?" answers George. "Is everything okay?"

"No!" she yells as her phone pings again.

"I'm doing homework," Jo calls from upstairs.

"I don't care what you're doing! Come down here now, or you're grounded for the rest of senior year!"

Laura knows she's overreacting, but what else can she do? She can't call Phil and ask for help. He'll have a field day with this. And probably reward Jo for her creative thinking. Laura walks into the kitchen as feet shuffle above her.

"You know you should set more tangible timelines with your punishments, Ma. I read it in that book you have in the bathroom." George leans back and teeters on a chair at the kitchen table.

Laura rolls her eyes and makes a note to remove *What to Expect When You're a Single Parent* from the bathroom and to email the counselor at school to make sure George has been selected to take the gifted student tests.

Jo appears wearing her headphones like she can't be bothered to hear whatever Laura has to say. Laura reaches over and pulls them off.

"Hey!" Jo complains.

"Did you put me on Buoy?" Laura stands with her hands on her hips, waiting for an answer.

Meg pops up in the doorway behind Jo. Meg probably isn't completely innocent in this scenario. Every villain has a good wingman.

"Yep!" Jo says with a smile. "Figured you must be curious about it, since you were snooping around on the app yesterday."

She is curious. Sue her. It's been eighteen months since Phil walked out the door. Part of her thinks it's time to look at her options. But she is not ready to get on the site. The other day was an exploratory mission to see the app everyone in the PNW raves about and to see if her ex is using it. And anyway, when she is ready to get on it, she wants to do it! Not have a profile created by her offspring.

"I just wanted to support you," Jo says, her voice dripping in sugar.

Before Laura can yell bullshit, she calms herself down with some box breathing and remembers that the infamous book says to count to ten before reacting in anger.

"I'm not sure I need that kind of support." Maybe if they could arrange for a prince to come riding down the driveway on his white horse and sort the recycling, she would accept that help. But looking for a date in such a public fashion is not her style. She already has a neon sign flashing above her head. The last thing she needs is to be objectified by men on an app. Laura blows a few strands of hair off her forehead. Is that her old age talking, or is the app the only way to do things nowadays? She'll have to give it some thought.

Meg takes a step forward. "We only want you to be happy."

Meg's words sting like the buzz of a too early alarm. All kinds of thoughts whirl through Laura's head. The first being: Why do the kids think she's not happy? She can't let them think she's not content being their mom or with her current life, even if she doesn't love the drudgery of the morning routine, taking out the garbage, and nagging them to do all the things.

"I am happy! I love being your mom."

"Duh," says George. "We know that!"

"We just want you to have someone other than us," says Meg.

Dagger straight to the heart. Moms aren't meant to be the needy ones. She's supposed to have it all together and be there for her kids. Her kids are not supposed to take care of her.

"You deserve a hot piece of meat," replies Jo.

And they're definitely not supposed to think about her sex life. Nothing that's going on in Laura's life goes by the playbook. She has to stop reading all those ridiculous parenting books and believing there's a right way for things to go.

"Hubba hubba," adds George.

Laura's cheeks grow red as she glances at her phone. "Well, good job on the profile pic, but I do not need the island calling me a frisky cat herder."

"Oh! I can fix that!" Jo yanks the phone from Laura's hands.

Laura looks at Jo. "There's going to be some kind of punishment for this."

Jo glances at the phone and then at Laura. "I'm sorry. I was mad. I'll cook dinner every night for the rest of the month."

A punishment that doesn't punish Laura. Perfect.

"Deal. Cooked—no takeout."

Laura takes her phone from Jo and goes upstairs to her safe haven—her bathroom in the primary. The kids have been afraid to come near it ever since Meg walked in on Laura shaving her nether regions. In hindsight, there was probably a less scarring way to teach them to knock before opening a door, but if nothing else, it was effective.

Laura sits on the edge of her bathtub, phone in hand, and scrolls through her messages. A contract to review. Updated pet custody agreement. Yes, it's a thing. And a message from a Henry Walter that ends with a vegetable emoji.

Why would someone use vegetables to sign off?

Laura googles "what does a purple vegetable symbolize?" She gasps when the search results come up. She is not tough enough for this digital world. She sticks her phone in her vanity drawer and heads back down to the kids.

on thin pines

Tippy Meadowcroft

"Tippy, you know you can't lock your bike to the front railing anymore." Gordon, the manager of Thin Pines Country Club, stands at the entrance to the club.

"Where would you like me to put her? The bike rack is clear on the other side of the courts."

"I know. That's so bicycles don't clutter the entrance of the club."

"I have one bike—singular—and as it's February, I'm willing to bet there won't be any other intrepid riders tonight. And it's dark enough that no one can see Bertha tucked in over here."

Gordon shakes his head and moves inside. The Thin Pines Decorum Committee emailed Tippy last week about where she should park Bertha, and she will comply on busy summer evenings, but tonight it doesn't matter. And Tippy Meadowcroft hates nothing more than rules that are made for ridiculous reasons.

Tippy opens the heavy oak doors and strolls into the foyer of Thin Pines. No one's at the baby grand, confirming it's a quiet night. The crystal chandelier reflects off the surface of the piano. Tippy marches through the dining room and into the lodge-like bar, all dark wood, leather stools, and dim lights.

Calder, clad in a button-down shirt showing off her glowing décolletage and a smile not fitting a person who's headed into a meeting, greets Tippy in the bar. She's sipping a martini straight up with three green olives stuffed with blue cheese.

"We're going to be in here tonight. You can set up in the corner if you'd like."

Tippy walks over to a two-top next to a table set for four and sets up camp. Her table tripod will work well at this angle. Other than the bartender, there's no one but her and Calder in the bar area.

Volunteer of the year, Amanda Willows, arrives, and Tippy can't help but notice she should have added a bit more concealer to cover the dark circles under her eyes.

Tippy films Laura Prescott arriving in glasses and a baseball cap—like she's hiding from the paparazzi, or her ex-husband. Laura tucks an unusually stray blond hair behind her ear and fusses with the waistband on her jeans as she sits at the table.

"Have they loosened the dress code?" Amanda looks at Laura. "I didn't think Thin Pines allowed baseball caps in the bar area."

"No one else is here. I'm sure Gordon will make an exception this time," Calder says in a deep voice barely loud enough for Gordon, standing in the doorway, to hear.

Tippy chuckles to herself. She is also well aware that her overpriced utility khakis may qualify as cargo pants. She dares Gordon to question her and try to get her to change into the generic elastic-waist khakis they've reserved for dress code violators.

Amanda puts a hand on Laura's arm. "You've had some excitement," she says sweetly, but Laura furrows her brow and sets her hands on the table.

"How did you hear about that?" Laura cross-examines.

"Dance class. All the moms were saying how great you look in your profile picture." Amanda shrugs.

"Let's straighten this out. I did not put myself on the dating app; Jo did."

Tippy looks at her phone to make sure she's live and recording.

"Apparently the kids want me to find love. Maybe they're hoping I'll stop harassing them about homework if I'm preoccupied." Laura uses humor to deflect.

"Bless their hearts," says Calder, while Amanda laughs hard and stops abruptly with a single glance from Calder. "But are you ready for this next era?"

Laura raises her eyebrows "Possibly? I'm not sure I want to do it so publicly. I haven't dated since I was in college and things were more organic then. Other than our food, nothing's organic nowadays."

Amanda nods eagerly.

"I don't know if the app is an appropriate way to search for love." Laura straightens her cap.

Calder cocks her head to the side. "You might need to get with the times. Have you had a lot of matches so far?" Calder purses her lips.

Laura lets out a sigh as her shoulders fall. "Well, I'm learning a lot about the size of everyone's eggplant."

Amanda gasps and covers her mouth.

Laura continues. "It's clear the world is filled with perverts."

"Perverts? Like, on Greensea?" Amanda chokes out.

Tippy zooms in on Amanda's wide eyes.

"Not sure where they're from, but I'm sure Greensea has its fair share," the knowledgeable lawyer says.

Tippy clocks that fact and vows to check out Buoy for herself when she gets home. Might be another source for her gossip columns.

"How's dating life going for you? Have you found anyone interesting?" Laura turns the tables.

Calder crosses her arms and stares at the ceiling. "Let me just say, dating is not easy on an island. You might need to set your sights farther afield."

"I get it! After living here for all these years, I know everyone and their complicated legal histories!" Laura complains.

"We do, and they know us." Calder winks.

"But you never know when the next Golden Bachelor will need a new house," Amanda laughs.

A gust of wind reaches the bar, announcing Mayor Nickerbottom's arrival. Tippy groans in the corner. Calder sits up straighter. And Amanda takes out her notebook and pastes on a smile.

"Good evening, ladies. Thank you for taking time from your busy lives to be here," he says as he plods to the table, opting to remain standing instead of sitting with them. "I outlined the broad details at the meeting but wanted to take a moment to take a deeper dive into the situation. The state is ready to close the galley. As you know, they've said we would need fifty thousand dollars. I need you all to get the inside scoop on the galley to inform your fundraising. People don't open their wallets for balance sheets. They open them for stories."

Three faces stare back at him, unsure of what he's suggesting.

"So?" asks Laura. "What are you implying?"

"You need to find the stories. You need to meet the people who work there. See what your fellow islanders enjoy when they're there. Then your appeal for the money will have a heart."

Calder gently places her hand on the table and scoots her readers atop her head. "Mayor Nickerbottom, you know the three of us have been using the ferry for decades. We understand what it is."

"Understanding it isn't the same as telling the story, Calder." Laura says. "He's asking us to turn the work into a narrative."

"I know you like your ferry pours and your pretzels. But do you know how hard Leo works to keep the chowder filled?" The mayor straightens his tie.

"Why would we care?" asks Amanda.

"Just like when you raise money for Greensea Elementary and you tell people what the teachers need and why—that's the story I need you to create for the galley."

"How do you suggest we go about this?" Laura asks.

"Great question!" He claps his hands. "I've arranged for all three of you to work in the galley for the 7:05 a.m. sailing. It's the busiest, and quite frankly the one with the lowest alcohol sales, so I don't have to worry about getting any of you alcohol server permits. But you can still get up close and personal and see how every aspect of it works."

"When would you like us to do this?" Calder chimes in.

"Next Monday."

"But I have a deposition." Laura flicks through the calendar on her phone.

"And I have a closing." Calder places both hands in front of her.

"Monday is 'Read With Your Favorite Stuffie Day' at school," pleads Amanda.

Tippy snorts in the corner.

"Do you want to tell all of Greensea that none of you have enough time and the galley is donezo?" Mayor Nickerbottom tilts his head to the side as the women shake their heads. "The sooner we tackle this, the sooner it will be over."

Tippy moves around in her chair in the corner. "The people are speaking! They don't want you to quit."

"The people?" asks Laura, raising her eyebrows. "How many people are you talking about?"

"I don't like to break the fourth wall, but we have a dozen

people out there watching. And I'm sure the rest of the island will watch later. Someone named Islandman commented and said you have to continue for the good of the island."

Calder smooths her hair, straightens the neckline of her button-down, and gives her best smile for the camera.

"Islandman is Thomas. His galley meals are the highlight of his day." Amanda rolls her eyes. She looks straight at the camera. "Put Cleo to bed, Thomas!" She swallows another hiccup.

Tippy tsks. "You can't speak directly to the camera, Amanda!"

"Thomas and his need for ferry food should not be the reason we sacrifice so much of our time to this task." Laura displays her courtroom demeanor, again.

"Thomas is the quintessential islander commuting back and forth to the city via ferry every day. Hundreds do the same thing." Amanda purses her lips.

"What!" Tippy exclaims in the corner. "Anonymous-Greensea says not to leave this important task to a bunch of whiney women! The nerve!"

Eyes squint and glare toward the camera. Scowls grow. Nostrils flare. Mayor Nickerbottom disregards the idea with a flick of his hand and speaks first. "The group assembled before me is highly capable." He waves his hand toward the camera, dismissing the invisible commenter. "Given the revenue from food services on the ferry, we know it's something people want and need."

"We are not whining. Simply getting more information." Calder looks directly at the camera. "If the revenue is so high, then why are they threatening to close it?"

"Do you want me to read the party line again?" Mayor Nickerbottom pushes his glasses up his nose while Calder shakes her head.

"I'd like an honest answer," she says.

The mayor's shoulders slump. "It's the easiest way to

increase the efficiency of the boat without looking at any other issues."

"Let's be real," starts Amanda. "The Greensea galley causes them too much trouble, so we have to prove it earns its space on the boat, even if it's inconvenient on paper."

"Exactly, Amanda!" Mayor Nickerbottom claps. "And on that note, I'll see you all on Monday morning."

Tippy stops recording as the women stand to leave.

———

The house is quiet when Tippy returns home. Dave's at The Old Owl for Trivia Night, arguing about useless facts with his brothers.

Bear meets her at the door, tail wagging like he's been waiting for a hambone. She hangs her bike helmet on its hook, slips off her shoes, and pours herself a mug of chamomile and lemon balm from the too-hot tap.

She opens her laptop out of habit. Just a peek.

The footage fills the screen. Laura hiding under her cap. Calder's calm, cool, and questioning attitude, all while she sips on her drink. Amanda's dismissal of her husband.

Tippy rewinds. Plays it again. Slows it down.

She sits up, tea forgotten. Each woman pulls the frame toward her in turn. Different stakes. Different secrets. Different ways of wanting to be right.

She drags clips into a timeline, weaving the town meeting footage in between. She has reaction shots, pauses, and well-timed sighs.

She even creates bios for each of the women.

Laura Prescott: I wear the pants at home, and in the courtroom.

Amanda Willows: I'm the manager of minions and CEO of cuddles.

Calder Cunningham: I hold the keys to your dreams.

The cursor blinks at the bottom of the screen like it's daring her to keep going.

Tippy glances at the clock. Dave will be home soon.

Without thinking about it too much more, she uploads the video to her Greensea Gazette account.

greensea gazette

Islanders,

We've come a long way from the days of posting updates about neighbors on bulletin boards around the island. In case you live under a rock, I've created a Youtube channel to take a deeper look as some of your favorite women attempt to save the ferry galley. I'm sure the tech-savvy teenagers in your life can help you find it if you don't know how. You're not going to want to miss it!

Since it seems to be all the rage amongst the island Gen X crowd, let's take a look at the newest app Buoy. Created by two best friends in Seattle, the dating app aims to match people based on their PNW interests. Think outdoor sports (rock climbing or kayaking), foodie tastes (raw bar or whiskey), and books (romance or lit fic). The question they ask to find your most suitable match: What do you do in the Big Dark? Genius! The national apps may have a bigger reach, but if you're single in our neck of the woods, Buoy is a life preserver for your love life. You might even see some of the esteemed members of the Save the Ferry committee on there.

But enough about technology for the moment. The Boy Scouts would like to apologize to all the hikers in the Grand Greensea Forest this past weekend. It seems Leader Thompson's lost walkie-talkie decided to make breathing noises until the batteries died. Officer Frank searched the lower trail until the walkie-talkie was located. To the two moms on the trail, you weren't being followed by a sex offender. Also, we checked your pace on the community running page, and you seemed to slow down after you thought you were being chased by a heavy breather. What's that about?

xoxo,
GG

one potato, two potato

Amanda Willows

Amanda Willow's alarm blares at 5 a.m. Even the sun has another two hours before it gets up. She takes a deep breath and reaches for her phone, which is resting on top of an aspirational to-be-read pile. For the umpteenth time, Amanda watches Tippy's latest video. The introduction montage rivals the ones on her favorite shows. Is there anything Tippy can't do? Gossip reporter, pickleball instructor, Fit Greenies leader, and now add film editor to her resume. The meeting's been cut down to a few minutes, but somehow with the glances and exchanges, the edit reads between the lines.

Much to her delight, there are very few shots of Amanda with a double chin, but live-action filming is another item for Amanda to add to her long list of things to worry about. And she keeps it in the forefront of her mind as she gets up and ready for the day.

She is not a mom who goes to Pilates—the reformer is intimidating on its own; add in a room filled with women and it's too much. Or a running one—islanders don't run casually; it's ultra marathons uphill both ways. And she doesn't play tennis or pickleball, because games that focus on individual skill stress her out. Instead, Amanda rides the stationary bike that's tucked in the corner of her bedroom—the one that also serves as a clothes rack. She does what she can on her own, occasionally trying a workout video she sees on Instagram. Because of her lackadaisical habits, she uses her clothes to hide what she fears may be perceived as a multitude of sins.

With great hopes that dropping Cleo off at school will make Thomas realize Amanda's work at home is hard and worthwhile, she leaves the house and heads to the ferry terminal to prepare for her 7:05 shift.

The ferry terminal is bustling with islanders heading into Seattle for work. Several people in scrubs—can't let anyone forget they are doctors—men in stretchy khaki pants and insulated vests, and women in long dark coats stand in the terminal waiting for the ferryboat to board. A movement to her right catches Amanda's eye, and she spots Tippy filming her arrival.

Great. It's started already.

Amanda attempts to press the wrinkles out of her overalls, then pulls at her low pony, trying to make it less messy and more presentable. Amanda has mastered her pose and smile for still photos, but she has not done so for video yet. That's another level of concentration and attention she's not sure she has. She's certain the cracks in her facade will be evident if the camera focuses on her too much. But, at the moment, her desire to help and be needed outweighs her worry about what may end up online.

"Morning, Tippy."

"Avoid talking to me if I'm filming," Tippy commands.

Amanda nods and approaches the coffee counter to buy a cup of coffee.

"Next," says the man behind the counter. Amanda glances at the menu.

"Ummm..."

"Order or move on. Ferry's coming!" the cashier says.

Flustered, she orders a plain cup of coffee with nothing in it.

Amanda looks at the black liquid, sighs, and decides to add creamer and sugar when they get into the galley. She needs to get better about saying what she wants outside of the house, and with that in mind, she edges over to join the rest of the group.

"Is that video the kind of thing we can expect to see every day?" asks Calder.

"Oh, yeah. I'll edit little snippets to keep people informed."

"You're doing a little more than informing," comments Laura. "You're creating your own narrative."

"All in good fun." Tippy laughs. "The views are great and obviously it will boost the cause."

After the ferry unloads, the women make their way down the ramp to the boat, passing the line of islanders waiting to board. The regulars whisper as this group of women seemingly cuts the line. But the lead galley worker, Esther, greets them at the end of the ramp, giving them the legitimacy they require.

"Good morning, gals! You ready to see what we do?"

They nod, like sailors agreeing to a route on a map they don't quite trust. Clearly, Esther has consumed more coffee than any of them has.

"Been working on the ferry for thirty-seven years, and I've never had anyone shadow me."

"Has the state ever threatened to remove funding for the galley?" Laura asks.

Esther shakes her head. "Never. I'm an I'll-believe-it-when-I-see-it gal. Can't imagine they'll shut down people's favorite part of the boat."

They follow Esther onto the stern, past all the seating, and into the galley. The galley is a semicircle cafeteria with food on either side and four cash registers at the exits. The refrigerators are stocked with yogurts, hummus, energy drinks, and kombucha. Toward the back sit containers with hot food—pretzels, tater tots, and soup. At the moment, none of it sounds appetizing to Amanda. She heads toward the condiment bar and finds some cream and sugar to sweeten her too-dark morning elixir.

"First thing, you'll all need to put on a hairnet or cover your hair in some way."

Esther holds out a bouquet of hairnets. Unless she's suddenly become European chic, a hairnet is not going to fly with Amanda's look. Laura, already wearing a brown trucker hat, shakes her head in a pass. "Will my hat do?" she asks.

"Yep! A hat is fine," answers Esther.

Calder unties a silk scarf from her purse and pulls her brown hair into a perfect chignon. Amanda swerves her head from side to side and eyes a glass display case filled with green Ferry Girl hat souvenirs. $34—that's hard to justify. She claims one anyway. A hairnet is a no go if Tippy's going to be filming the whole time.

"I'll pay for it at the end of the day," she says to no one in particular.

"Ladies, the 7:05 is our busiest boat. You're each going to shadow someone. Keep up or move to the side."

Esther points to Laura. "You're with Carl and Nina at the espresso stand."

"You're at the cash register." She points to Calder.

"And you're in the back with Nancy."

Amanda strolls behind the main counter to check out food prep while the other women move to their assigned spots. Amanda adjusts her posture as she watches Tippy circle the area, filming on her phone.

Nancy stands at a long metal table, shoveling tater tots into paper boats.

"Hi! I'm Amanda." She reaches her hand out, but Nancy

keeps working. "Have you worked on the ferry for a long time?" she asks, trying to find the narrative for the mayor.

"Load these up in the hot holding station."

Amanda stands there, and Nancy looks at her. "What? Oh! Me?" Obviously, Nancy is singularly focused on what she's doing.

"Yes," she says, and Amanda scoops up two containers of tater tots.

"Where is the heated station?"

New places stress Amanda out. Greensea Elementary is her territory. She knows the ins and outs. The inner workings of the ferry galley are not familiar.

Nancy glares at her. "Ever buy food in the galley before?"

Amanda nods.

"It's the place that keeps everything warm."

Duh. Amanda takes the first set of tater tots and places them in the display. She goes back for more and on the return bumps into a ferry passenger. Tater tots scatter to the ground.

"Oops! Excuse me." Her cheeks burn as she bends down to pick them up.

"Amanda Willows? Is that you?" asks a black haired woman dressed in a camel-colored wool coat.

"Oh, hi, Kendra." Amanda can't help but stare. Kendra is so put together. Her skin is dewy, her long lashes frame her brown eyes, and there's not a curl out of place on her entire head. And she smells like a Parisian garden. If Amanda were at home right now, she'd be in her pajama carpool outfit, but Kendra looks like she's about to take on the board room. Kendra has three kids at Greensea Elementary. How does she look so carefully curated?

Kendra puts a hand on Amanda's forearm. "It's so great you got a job on the ferry!"

Amanda pulls away. "Oh, no." Her cheeks flush. "I'm just here to volunteer today for, um, the, you know, Save the Ferry committee."

Kendra cocks her head to the side like she has no idea what Amanda's talking about. Obviously, Kendra had more important things to do than attend the town meeting. It's a familiar refrain: issues that are of the utmost importance to Amanda but don't even seem to be on anyone else's radar. School book fair without inexpensive plastic tchotchkes? No one cares. School festival with face painting using non-estrogen-containing paints? Definitely no one cares to source them, and assumes someone else will. So it doesn't surprise Amanda that Kendra's mind is not filled with the latest civic concerns of the island.

"Ma'am," yells the lady with the tater tots. "Let's go! Got more to load!"

Amanda watches Kendra sashay to the cash register with her yogurt. For once in her life, Amanda would like to look so polished and confident. But for now, she's a blushing, babbling mom who can't put two words together—let alone an outfit that appeals to more than grade school kids.

Amanda makes her way back to the ever-growing pile of tater tots. Mayor Nickerbottom has tasked them with studying the galley, but with everything moving so quickly, it's hard to understand what's going on. And plus, the Sound is choppy today, making the boat rock. Amanda holds onto the metal counter.

"On to oatmeal next!" The woman scoops oatmeal into paper cups and has Amanda place it in the same warmer.

For the first time today, Amanda has a tiny idea—an oatmeal bar with fresh fruit and all the accoutrements.

"Wouldn't it be great if there was an oatmeal bar with organic toppings?" Amanda comments to Nancy.

Nancy turns up her lip. "This is not a five-star restaurant. This is a mode of transportation that happens to have food."

Amanda takes that as a no. The story she's gathering is that they don't want her help.

"How's the chowder looking?" Nancy bellows.

Amanda inches toward the container of soup. Why is anyone having clam chowder for breakfast? She opens the lid and is hit with the smell of warm clams and cream. She throws her hand over her mouth as she practically gags into it. "It's fine. Plenty in there."

Hmmm. She never gets seasick. Why does she still feel this way?

She will get to the bottom of this dodgy stomach tomorrow. But today's mission is to survive.

useful or invisible

Laura Prescott

At first glance, Laura thinks the sprawling silver-and-black coffee machine in front of her can't be that different from her white plastic Mr. Coffee. At second glance, she realizes she is wrong. The one in front of her swallowed her Mr. Coffee and spit it out with all the bells and whistles.

"Either make yourself useful or make yourself invisible," Carl barks from the cash register.

A bead of sweat pools under Laura's hat. Nina, the barista, slides in beside her on the left.

"Just steam the milk for me," Nina whispers, handing her a small metal cup. The counter is lined with at least six containers of milk. Laura notes the absence of oat milk. And goat milk. The mayor must have been here.

"I'll tell you which kind for each cup. You pour it in the metal pitcher and stick the nozzle in to steam it."

Easy. This won't be that hard.

"Have you worked here for a bit?" Laura asks Nina.

"Just about a year." Nina smiles. "You get used to the pace... and Carl. He's a softie under that tough exterior."

Orders stack up fast. Two percent. Nonfat. Whole. Soy. Laura discovers that nothing steams as well as whole milk and nothing misbehaves quite like soy. She finds a rhythm. This isn't so bad. Maybe she is competent outside the courtroom.

"Two percent!" Nina calls.

Laura reaches for the milk and senses someone standing directly in front of her. Her gaze catches on a pair of black pants, travels up a perfectly pressed white shirt with bars on the shoulders, and finally lands on the lightly stubbled face of the captain. Hazel eyes, bright and amused, like fog lights cutting through a morning crossing.

Captain McHottyPants. Of course.

"Eyes off the captain! The ferry isn't a floating dating app!" Carl has no mercy and seems to be an avid reader of the *Greensea Gazette*.

"You learning the ropes back here?" he asks. Dimples appear, as if summoned.

"Umm. Yeah." Her voice comes out like one of her teenaged daughters'.

With the carton of two percent in one hand and the metal cup in the other, Laura plunges the steamer down.

Into the milk carton.

The machine shrieks. Milk explodes. Hot droplets splatter her face, Nina's apron, and the captain's once-pristine shirt.

"You've got to be kidding me," Carl snaps from the cash register. "I knew you Salty Mamas would cause more trouble here than you're worth. Go. Get cleaned up."

Laura's cheeks ignite. She bolts from the coffee closet and nearly collides with the captain, who's waiting at the door holding a wad of napkins.

"Here," he says, handing them over. "Sorry. I didn't mean to distract you."

How chivalrous.

"No, that one's on me." Laura wipes her face. "I'm the idiot who tried to steam milk directly in the carton."

He reaches up and dabs the brim of her hat. He's close enough that she catches a hint of aftershave. Eucalyptus and pine trees.

When was the last time she was around a man who wore aftershave? Do they still call it that? She'd swipe right. Or up. Or whatever the people do on that app.

She tilts her head to the ceiling. *Get a hold of yourself, Laura!* Ever since Jo put her on the app, the idea of dating has been jumping around in her head.

"Sorry, I was distracted," she adds. "Thought I saw a client behind you."

His mouth curves into a full-toothed smile.

"Did you at least get your coffee?" she asks, turning her gaze to the counter to force herself to stop staring at him.

"Nina's making it now."

"Guess I'm better in the courtroom than I am in the galley."

"Too soon to call it," he says, winking. "It's only your first day."

"Captain, latte's up!"

He turns toward the counter. "Good luck," he says over his shoulder as he heads toward the bridge.

She's going to need more than luck. And she also needs something to quell the butterflies in her stomach. *Jeez.* It's not the first time she's been around a man in a uniform.

She slips back into the coffee closet. "How about I write the orders on the cups?"

Nina and Carl exchange a look, then nod in sync.

"One more strike and you're outta here," says Carl, punching the air like a baseball umpire.

Fortunately for Laura, it's only a thirty-two-minute crossing.

tip jar

Calder Cunningham

"Think you've seen enough to give it a go on your own?" asks Esther, moving to the side of the cash register.

"No problem at all." Calder used a similar checkout system at Greensea High School when she collected tickets for a play. How different can this really be? And after watching Esther use it, she's confident she has the skillset to manage it on her own.

"Scan the item. If it doesn't have a barcode, then search for it. Hit total and you're done. Easy as pie." Esther steps to the side, and Calder sidles up.

She straightens her vintage Hermès scarf she found in a market in Palm Springs and smiles at the first customer in front of her.

A yogurt. Easy. She rings it up, and the person taps their phone on the pad. She gives herself a pat on the back for figuring it out so easily.

"Guess I'll have to start bringing my own brown bag breakfast," the next customer grunts as they walk away.

"No! No! Don't worry. The ladies and I are handling it!"

Calder calls after them and smiles. "We'll make sure the galley is around forever."

"Just stick to ringing them up," says Esther, smacking a piece of gum next to her.

"Good morning, Calder," says a smooth voice in front of her. She looks up from the cash register. Phil, Laura's ex.

"How are you today?" he asks as she tries to locate the muffin on the screen.

"Fine." She's not about to engage anyone else in conversation. Especially with a line of six people behind him.

"That's a manual entry," sighs Esther.

Calder flips the muffin over and notices an orange $5.99 sticker. She types it in without the decimal point and the register flashes $599.00.

"Scoot." Esther hip-checks Calder out of the way.

"Fantastic that you three are taking up this cause," Phil says, like it's a charity auction and not people's jobs. Phil sticks his hand in his pocket, giving no hint of leaving. He takes out a ten-dollar bill and places it in the tip jar. Calder rolls her eyes.

"Keep moving, buddy. There's a line of people behind you," Esther reprimands after she corrects Calder's error.

He chuckles and says, "I'll be in touch later."

In touch? No, thank you. Calder does not need to exchange any words with the person who left her friend high and dry.

The ferry rocks. Calder clutches the register to steady herself and watches in horror as a beer rings up with the oatmeal.

"Esther…"

With a huff, Esther moves in and fixes the next mistake, so it reads oatmeal $7.50.

"You three are in charge of saving our jobs? Can't even ring up an oatmeal properly." Esther's muttering to herself, but just loud enough for Calder to hear. "Sitting up in Thin Pines acting like saviors." Esther knits her brow. "Nothing like a bunch of wealthy women thinking they can save the world."

Calder's chest prickles. They were asked to do this. They didn't volunteer on their own.

"It was the mayor who decided we were the ones to raise the money. We didn't volunteer for this."

"Just the same. He should have come to us."

Calder looks at the flashing register in front of her. Esther's right. No one asked the people who would lose the most.

eureka

Tippy Meadowcroft

Gold freaking mine!

Tippy giggles to herself as she films the interactions. This video is going to be everything she imagined. The way Laura sputtered milk all over herself and the captain. Amanda gagging over the clam chowder. Calder getting the what-for from Esther. Her ensuing blush and flustered face. Tippy's tempted to dig up the emails from the producers who've politely rejected her for years. She can already picture the subject line: You said no to this? There's no way they could reject this pricelessness. Instead, she'll show them. Episode by episode. Brands aren't built overnight. They're built with chaos, consistency, and a bit of manipulation. She pops a piece of popcorn in her mouth.

The ferry docks, and the people pour off. The group has been given rare permission to stay on the boat between sailings.

Reveling in the few quiet minutes, the women take a break. Laura, Calder, and Amanda take a seat at a booth with Tippy. The engine quiets as the ferry idles and ferry workers complete their requisite check for stragglers, garbage, and unattended baggage.

"That was brutal," says Laura.

"Not a lot of love from the crew," adds Calder, letting her hair down and wiping her brow. "Tippy, you need to focus on the people who will lose their jobs if the galley closes."

Tippy furrows her brow. The ferry workers haven't agreed to be in her videos. Maybe she can share a post about them in GG.

Amanda rubs her neck, then her wrist, then presses a palm flat against her stomach like it's misbehaving.

They don't even notice Tippy pointing the camera toward each of them as they speak.

"You have the easiest job!" complains Laura.

"Not everything's a competition." Calder checks her phone.

"Well, you didn't explode a container of milk all over yourself and the captain!" Laura puts her head on the table.

"We had a rush on drip coffee because no one wanted to risk ruining their outfits at the espresso bar," Calder coos.

"I had no idea how many tater tots were consumed before 9 a.m. And chowder? Who eats clams for breakfast?" Amanda leans her head against the plexiglass window.

"Are you okay?" Laura asks.

"I don't know. I, uh, I'm a little woozy just thinking about seafood. I might be a little seasick. Honestly, food in general hasn't sounded great for the last few days."

"Your color's drained from your cheeks," notes Calder.

Tippy zooms in on Amanda with steady hands and professional instincts. Medical moments always go viral.

"Here, lie down." Laura scoots out of the booth so Amanda can lie down.

"Put her feet up," says Calder. Laura eases Amanda's feet onto the table.

"Is she filming?" Calder points to Tippy.

"Of course she is," Laura complains. "Tippy! Stop filming and go grab her a banana and some saltines," Laura snaps.

"You go! I'm busy!"

Laura rises in a huff.

A ferry worker comes to the table. "You ladies okay?" He fumbles with his walkie-talkie and says, "We've got a Salty Mama down in the galley."

"What's with the Salty Mama nickname?" Tippy asks.

"Focus on Amanda, Tippy!" Calder chides.

Laura returns, hands Amanda a cracker packet, and pops open a water bottle.

"No one's down!" Amanda sits up slowly. "I'm fine! It's the thought of that...seafood." She drinks a sip of water.

"Have you eaten anything today?" Laura asks, and peels the banana.

Amanda whispers, "No."

"Have some banana," Calder insists.

Amanda nibbles the smallest possible bite, chewing like the banana might argue back. Tippy continues to film. There's no way she's stopping now.

As passengers begin to file onto the ferry for the next sailing, the captain approaches the table. "Ladies, is everyone okay?"

"I'm fine. I'm fine," Amanda insists. "I'm going to sit the next shift out. Laura, will you take over for me in the galley?"

"Absolutely." Laura nods her head. "Tippy you stay with Amanda in case she needs anything."

No prob. She knows she can film from right here.

Laura heads toward the galley.

"Need me to bring you any protective gear?" asks the captain.

Laura tugs the brim of her hat and continues into the galley. If only Tippy could see her cheeks.

Other than Calder knocking over the tip jar, scattering change all over the floor, the next sailing goes by without fanfare.

As the women disembark the ferry, looking like they've barely survived a Black Friday sale, Mayor Nickerbottom greets them.

"Well, ladies?" Mayor Nickerbottom beams and claps his hands together like he's about to announce the winner of the pie contest. "How was it?"

They're tired, and a little worse for wear, and all ready to return to their regular lives.

"Good." Tippy musters up the most sunshine.

"Fine," Calder and Laura reply in unison.

Amanda stays quiet.

"Why don't we have a quick meeting this week while your ideas are still fresh?"

Tippy notes the collective eye roll, because no one has time for this.

"Let's get it over with," says Amanda.

"Meet at The Salty Skein. The office got a complaint about a city meeting taking place at an elitist club," Mayor Nickerbottom adds.

After a day of spilled milk, gagging over chowder, and nearly fainting on a ferry bench, elitism is not the word any of them would have chosen. But Tippy smiles to herself. These women bring the drama wherever they go.

greensea gazette

Dear Islanders,

I accompanied the housewives as they volunteered in the galley on the 7:05 sailing and I learned a lot—other than the obvious: that Laura Prescott cannot operate machinery. Esther, who's been running the register since '92, knows Joe Russo is allergic to peanuts and looks out for cross-contamination. Carl, who runs the espresso stand, writes happy messages on Ms. Schmidt's cups as she heads into the city for her treatment. Darryll, who looks like he's patrolling for alcoholic beverages being consumed outside the galley area, is first aid certified—don't ask how we know. These people are doing more than ringing up your ferry pours, and to suggest their jobs are disposable removes a layer of onboard safety we currently rely on. We intend to make sure the people in Olympia don't sacrifice their jobs.

Speaking of government failures, Arrowhead Road is headed for a do-over. The city apologizes for the wayward paver that added unexpected topography to an otherwise flat stretch of asphalt. Those bonus speed humps were not, in fact, a feature. Ride your one wheeler somewhere else!

The city council plans to outlaw the "Honk if Your Child's Gifted" bumper stickers. The city understands they were intended to be a fundraiser but...honestly? Does someone need to explain one of the many reasons they're not a great idea? How did such a ridiculous idea come from a parent of a smart kid?

xoxo,
GG

birds and the bees

Amanda Willows

Still in her carpool outfit, Amanda stands in her kitchen and watches the latest edition of Tippy's *Housewives*—again. On screen, she looks smaller than she feels. A revelation she'll try to remember. But her smile always arrives half a second too late. Her eyes flick toward the exits, the ferry schedule board, the people walking behind the camera. She remembers exactly how her stomach felt then, tight and fluttering, but she hadn't realized it showed in her facial expressions. She wonders if the nerves she sees are apparent to the casual viewer.

She presses pause. Tippy has an eye for making nothing into something.

Amanda silenced Thomas' concerns last night about her medical episode being broadcast out in public. She argued people would have found out without the video, since it happened on the ferry. He mumbled about her picking up germs at the damn school, but forced her to put up her feet and take it easy, confirming he hadn't turned into a complete ogre. He even made Cleo's day when he declared it Cereal for Dinner Night.

Now parsing through the 106 comments on the video—even more than a post on the Greensea Islanders Facebook page—Amanda can see islanders are invested in this little series. Comments range from wondering if Calder's scarf is a fit hairnet to questioning Laura's legal eye if she isn't astute enough to know where to put the steamer. Someone says Salty Mamas are only good at ferry pours and not fit to save anything. What is this Salty Mama nickname? The vast majority of the comments are critical and have no faith in their abilities. Is it because they're women? Moms? Amanda isn't sure, but vows to prove them all wrong.

One comment from Greenanonymoussea catches Amanda's eye.

    Fainting is a natural response to the
    body's hormonal changes.

Hormonal changes? What hormonal changes? The commenter can't possibly think she's the same age as the other women in the group and going through perimenopause. Laura and Calder have a decade—at least—on Amanda. She opens the camera on her phone and looks at her face. Yes, the dark circles do emphasize the crow's feet. She holds down her part. Not one strand of gray in her black hair.

And then she holds her stomach like it's betrayed her. Not those hormonal changes. The opposite ones.

The tennis skirt. The abnormally warm, sunny day in January when Cleo was at a sleepover. The one time she agreed to play pickleball. Thomas and his frisky paws.

It hits her like a ferry coming in to dock.

She drinks a sip of coffee and then spits it out all over the counter. If she's pregnant, she can't have caffeine. She doesn't know if she should laugh or cry. But she does know she needs to buy a test. Grabbing her keys and her new Ferry Girl hat, she hightails it back to her minivan and heads to Greensea Drugs.

Amanda slinks up to the cash register, hoping no one will recognize her. She slides the test across the counter to the cashier, Thelma Welkins.

"Would you like a bag, dear?" Thelma asks.

"Absolutely!"

"That will be eight cents."

"Don't you have those little, tiny white bags?"

"We do. They're eight cents, Ms. Willows."

Amanda rolls her eyes. This godforsaken island charges for everything they can. But even worse, Thelma recognizes her. Are pharmacy workers held to the Hippocratic oath? She sure hopes so.

"Okay. Whatever. I'll take it."

Amanda pays for the test and blasts out the door without a goodbye. A rustling in the bushes next to her van catches her eye. A tuft of red hair signals Tippy Meadowcroft hiding in there, filming Amanda.

"Tippy! What are you doing here?" The branches part and Tippy emerges.

"Oh, hi! I saw your car and figured I'd get some footage." Tippy sways back and forth like she's a kid proving to Santa she's been angelic.

"Why me right now?" Amanda thinks about how she looks —call in the fashion police, she's beyond disheveled. She puts the bag behind her back, hoping Tippy hasn't noticed it.

"Because you're buying a pregnancy test, right?"

Shit. Leave it to Tippy to know everything.

"No!" she says, her brow knitting itself together.

Tippy cocks her head to the side. "Really? Then what's in the bag?"

"Okay. Fine. It is." Amanda steps toward her minivan. She supposes there's not much to hide at this point, since the whole world—or at least the island—already saw her nearly faint.

"Can I record you taking the test?"

Tippy has lost her mind. "No! Peeing on a stick is something for OnlyFans, not your little small-town video series."

Tippy's forehead creases. "Then will you at least text me the results?"

"Nope!" Amanda gets in her van to drive home.

———

With her dose of reality TV slightly delayed, Amanda sets her iPad on the bathroom counter and turns on an episode of *Real Housewives* before she opens the white paper bag. Her soul relaxes with the sound of the intro music.

She opens the box and wonders if the process has changed in the last eight years. It's still a pee on the stick situation, but looks like it doesn't take as long as it used to. Amanda unwraps the stick and squats over the toilet seat, hoping she doesn't pee too much on her hand. She sets the wand on the sink and watches the housewives arguing over coffee, which hits with renewed interest after watching Tippy's cut of them on the ferry. Clearly, Tippy's done her fair share of research and is taking this up a notch—even trying to get some B-roll of them around town.

The timer on her watch buzzes, and she looks at the stick. There's no mistaking what it says. A gigantic blue plus sign illuminates the window.

Pregnant. It's real. Not food poisoning from fruit leathers.

She sits on the bathroom floor with her head against the vanity. She loves being a mom. Cleo is a walking embodiment of her heart outside her body. She's the best of everything about Amanda. Her single crowning pride and joy. Another Cleo will be nothing short of amazing.

But she'd be lying if she said she wasn't worried that she may be the only one on cloud nine about this new development. It will delay her ability to work and it will be an extra, unexpected expense. She taps his name on her phone.

Of course. No answer.

She could use their 9-1-1 signal and give him a double ring, but she'll still be pregnant later. She can tell him when he gets home.

Her thoughts are interrupted by the iPad and one housewife calling another a bitch before storming out of the coffee shop. At least the Greensea moms don't do things like that. As if on cue, Tippy texts.

Tippy: Positive or negative?

Without thinking, she sends back a positive, gets up, and curls up in bed. The list of chores for today can wait. It's important to rest, right?

———

The shrill ring of her phone wakes her from a sound sleep.

"You're pregnant?" Thomas asks, already wound tight.

Amanda squints at her phone. "Yes...how do you know?"

"It's all over the Internet."

Damn Tippy.

"Sorry." She wipes her cheek. "I didn't mean for that to happen. I called but you didn't answer."

"Yeah, my boss has had me running around all morning."

Still, she knows he shouldn't have found out with the rest of Greensea.

"Sorry. I wasn't feeling great, and Tippy saw me at the store and—" She stops herself, then tries again, softer. "But...we're pregnant."

His silence fills the air.

"Are you upset?" she asks.

"No," he says too quickly. "No, I mean—I love Cleo. Obviously. And a sibling is...that's great."

Amanda sits up, then immediately regrets it and sinks back into the pillow. "Then what is it?"

He exhales. "Work's just... not great right now."

"Not great how?"

"There are layoffs. In every department. Every day it's something new."

Amanda blinks. "Okay, but—you've been there forever."

"That doesn't matter."

"It has to matter a little."

"It doesn't," he says again, sharper this time. Then, quieter, "They don't care how long you've been there."

She presses her lips together. "Is that why you keep talking about me going back to work?"

He sighs.

"Yeah," he says. "I just want us to be covered in case anything happens."

Why didn't he tell her? He's been carrying this around like a second phone in his pocket, buzzing nonstop.

"But I'm pregnant," she says, the words landing heavier now. "It's not exactly...ideal timing to go back to work."

"I know. But we don't even have three months of expenses saved, Amanda," he says. "We're not like everyone else on Greensea."

Her chest tightens. It always comes down to her feeling different than the other islanders—and money is usually the reason.

She swallows, then tries to force some lightness. "Well, being proactive would've been keeping everything in your pants when I was wearing that tennis skirt. I'm already pregnant, so unless you've got a time machine, I'm not sure what the plan is here, bud."

Silence from the other end of the phone.

"We'll put your bonus in savings this year. We don't have to do a beach trip." Amanda feels a flicker of pride at landing on a solution.

"The rumor is we might not get bonuses this year."

Great. There goes that idea. Amanda closes her eyes. "We'll figure it out," she says, softer now. "If something happens, we'll deal with it."

"We need a plan before that."

"We'll make one," she says, but there's an edge now. "Just... not this second."

He sighs—again.

She exhales. "I'm really tired."

"Yeah," he says.

Amanda hangs up and pulls the covers over her head. She pictures herself in scrubs again, name badge clipped on, like trying on a version of herself she packed away to be a mom.

She comes up for air after a few minutes and scrolls social media for Tippy's announcement. She finally finds it, with a recap of the footage from yesterday of Amanda passing out, and then the footage she got in the parking lot of Amanda coming out of the drugstore. Confetti falls on the screen and it says, "It's a baby!"

Oh, shoot! What if Cleo finds out before Amanda can tell her? Amanda scans her mental list of PTO moms at the school today. Is it someone who might mention it to Cleo? She can't take that risk.

She throws on her shoes and hightails it to the school. She parks and jumps out. Only then does she realize she's still in her carpool outfit from this morning—pajama pants and all. But time is of the essence. She bursts into the office.

"Quick, where is Cleo right now?"

"Mrs. Willows! Is everything okay?" asks Patricia.

"Yes, yes. I only need to speak with her for a second."

Her fingers pound her keyboard. "Art class!"

Patricia shoos her away. One of the perks of being PTO president is being able to appear at the school any time she wants. Amanda creaks open the door of the art room. "Sorry to interrupt. Can I borrow Cleo for a minute?"

Mrs. Spagnola looks up from an easel. "Sure thing!"

Cleo bounds out of the room. "Mommy! What are you doing here still dressed like that?"

Cleo laughs in the hallway.

"I needed to tell you something."

Cleo shrugs.

"Do you want to be a big sister?"

"What?" Cleo tugs on her ponytail.

Amanda leans down and grips both of Cleo's arms. "You're going to be a big sister!"

Cleo wriggles her arms out of Amanda's grasp.

"Mom! That's so embarrassing!"

"Embarrassing?" Amanda repeats. Why isn't anyone in this family happy about this?

"I'm eight! I'm almost double digits!" Cleo stomps her foot.

"And?" A class of tiny kindergarteners marches by on their way to recess, reinforcing that Cleo is older now. "Why does that matter?"

"The baby will be my age when I'm in high school! The baby will be George!"

George Prescott? What does Laura's son have to do with this?

"I thought you liked George?"

"I do! But he gets all the attention in the family. I've heard Jo is an afterthink."

Amanda can't help but chuckle.

"I think you mean afterthought. But Cleo, you will never be an afterthought. No matter what, you're my first born. The one who made me a mom. No one can ever take that away from you.

We've had eight years of just us. That's the most special thing we ever could have been given."

"Okay. Why'd you come to school to tell me?"

"I wanted you to hear it from me first."

Cleo shrugs and starts back into class, then turns around and looks Amanda up and down.

"Mom? Your breath doesn't smell so fresh."

At the close of the art room door, Amanda darts down the hallway, only to see Patricia waving her into the office.

"Amanda, Amanda!" She claps in excitement.

Obviously, the video is making the rounds. Amanda raises a hand and escapes the walls of the school. She has got to take a shower—and apparently brush her teeth.

clean-up on aisle five

Laura Prescott

Laura's phone pings mid-mediation with a notice from the city. Better not be another emergency meeting. She hardly has time for the Save the Ferry committee as it is.

> City of Greensea Island: High wind warning beginning at 5pm until tomorrow at 10am.

Shit. Great. She makes a mental note to stop at Island Grocers for some supplies, knowing full well the bananas will be gone by the time she gets there.

"Ms. Prescott, does that work for your client, or are you more concerned about what's happening on your phone?" She tucks her phone away and snaps back to what's in front of her—her client, Joy Hermanson, is suing her neighbor, Clyde Rickels, for creating a frog hatchery on his property. While it isn't illegal, it seems to violate the noise ordinance. How do they know? Imagine weeks of data collection on the Hermansons' deck using a decibel meter.

"I'm sorry. Would you mind repeating that, please?" Laura asks.

"Mr. Rickels agrees he will not introduce any new frogs into the habitat or create a mating ground next year. What's done is done this year, and we'd like to avoid your client's suggestion of euthanizing the frogs."

Joy was joking—Laura hopes—when she said she was going to throw a Tide Pod into the pond to poison the water. She looks at Joy who nods in agreement.

Fantastic, another island crisis averted. She shakes Joy's hand, closes her folders, and slips them into her bag.

Laura can't believe she gets paid to mediate arguments like this, but nothing really surprises her anymore. People like to argue over the most mundane things and nowadays the arguments escalate faster than one can imagine. Being a lawyer, a mom, and a divorcée on Greensea exposes her to the underbelly of island life.

Island Grocers is filled to the brim with islanders stocking up on what they deem to be essential for the next few days in case they lose power—an all-too-real event on this island. Today there seems to be a run on bananas—per usual—kombucha, and tofu. If her cart weren't a looking glass into her life, she'd be buying Doritos and rosé. But since she doesn't need any extra sideways glances today, she'll throw in a bunch of kale and hide what she really wants underneath it. But a bottle of rosé, who could fault her for that?

Turning the corner to pick up a bottle, Laura spots Barb Sherman.

"Hi, dear. How are you?" She touches Laura's shoulder.

"Managing." Laura shrugs.

"I remember the days when the kids were still in school. Utter chaos. They say the days are long and the years are short. Boy, as I look back now, that's true. But when I was trying to get four out the door in the morning, the minutes felt like I was drowning in quicksand."

Laura chuckles. Quicksand is an apt analogy for how she feels.

"I read the brand contract, Barb, and made a few adjustments. It's ready to sign now."

Barb Sherman has become a TikTok cooking sensation after an accidental Live. Now she has kitchen brands clamoring to work with her, and she and her husband, Tom, can finally afford to take well-earned vacations in their RV.

"Thank you!"

Laura reaches to a lower shelf and snags a bottle of wine.

"Fortitude." She glances at Barb and plops it in her cart. Barb laughs as they part ways.

Laura maneuvers toward the cereal aisle. A sugary treat will be a nice surprise for the kids and might even make tomorrow morning easier. While Island Grocers prides itself on its all natural and organic items, if one looks hard enough, the sinful items reveal themselves, usually hidden behind fiber and virtue. Laura pilfers through a free-standing display of shredded wheat to find the blueberry coated kind. She shuffles box after box aside, the display wobbling, and stretches toward the flash of blue she can see hiding in the back.

"Aha!" She snatches it toward her, sending the entire display collapsing around her ankles in an echoing avalanche. She's left standing in the middle of the aisle, victorious and alone, clutching the lone sugar-coated box. Hiding her treats is not going how she planned.

"Shit," she mutters, already crouching to pick things up, as if speed might erase witnesses.

An arm reaches down to help her. Laura takes in the forearm —defined muscles, dark hairs, and a small anchor tattoo on the inside of his wrist.

"So we meet again," says a deep voice next to her, because of course it does.

The tips of Laura's ears warm as she turns to look at McHottyPants, kneeling on the floor of Island Grocers.

"They always stick the good boxes in the back," he smiles. "Like a test."

"I know!" Nothing bonds two people faster than acknowledging mutual sugar seeking.

"Clean-up on aisle five," rings through the store intercom. "Next to Laura Prescott."

Laura closes her eyes in disbelief. Leaving out her name would have been kinder and saved her from the extra dose of embarrassment. But that's not Greensea's style.

A worker plods down the aisle with a broom and a full mop kit. "I'll take it from here."

"Just a few boxes," says McHotty as he stands and winks at Laura. "Don't think you need all the equipment."

"We've got to stop meeting like this," Laura says.

McHotty reaches his hand out. "Owen McHale."

"Laura Prescott," she replies as she shakes his hand—his fingers warm and gentle like something she's been missing. She holds on for a second longer than necessary.

"Here's to hoping our next encounter won't involve a clean-up." Owen looks at his watch. "Ohh! I've got to go. 'Til we meet again." He flashes his double-dimple smile before he's off.

She's frozen in the aisle with the clean-up aid stacking the boxes around her as she watches her knight in shining armor walk toward the checkout line. How very Greensea to run into the same person over and over again. Once they're in your orbit, it's hard to escape them.

"Excuse me," says the worker, removing boxes from around Laura while she peeks at her phone in her bag.

Yikes. Laura needs to leave, too, if she's going to make it to pick up George on time.

With not a minute to spare, she pulls up at school to pick up George. Some days, getting home is equivalent to climbing Mt. Rainier. Right now, she wants to put on comfy pants, charge all the devices, and sit on the couch watching trash TV.

"Georgie," she says as they walk through the door. "Homework first in case we lose power tonight."

"But Ma!"

"No buts, that's the way it's going to be."

George belly-laughs. "You said no butts."

She rolls her eyes as the door slams, and Meg and Jo appear in the kitchen. Jo drops her backpack. Meg places hers in the mudroom on her designated hook.

"Hey! Charge your devices in case we lose power," Laura instructs them. Meg comes over and gives her a kiss. Jo stands at the other side of the island.

"Tippy's videos are next level. Everyone's talking about you guys in the galley." Jo almost looks happy about it.

"I can't believe you exploded the milk like that," Meg laughs.

"Yeah, that part was cringe," says Jo. "But not as bad as Mrs. Willows passing out."

"Because she's pregnant!" adds George.

"What?" How come she's the last to know everything?

"Yeah, haven't you watched the latest?" Meg grabs a sparkling water from the fridge.

How was she supposed to watch the latest when she was working, at the store, and then picking up George? She thought Tippy was only putting these together when they were all together—at meetings. Jo thrusts her phone in front of her.

"Watch."

Sure enough, she watches Amanda walking out of Greensea Drugs and the ensuing montage.

Wow!

Laura exhales sharply. This is another level of intrusion. It's one thing to film the work of the ferry committee, but quite another to do this as well. Laura scrolls through the comments and sees dozens and dozens of congratulations.

"Can you see how many people have viewed this?"

Jo takes her phone back. "Five thousand, four hundred and thirty-nine."

Five thousand people? "That's a lot, right?"

"Yeah, not bad, especially since it's only been up a couple of hours." Jo gets a snack. "The views on your video might help you on Buoy."

Laura doesn't want any help on Buoy.

"You know Dad's on like every app," she continues.

In fact, Laura didn't know this. But she had a hunch. She stopped looking for Phil on Buoy when she found Jo. They've been separated for a while, and she doesn't expect that he's twiddling his thumbs. She shrugs.

"You need to actually use the profile I made for you," Jo urges like it's a race. "That thing is prime real estate."

"Honey, I've got a lot on my plate. I'm not sure I can add one more thing."

"Let's at least look to see if you have a match."

"Okay. Let me just get a few things done and dinner started." Laura has zero interest in her matches on Buoy, but she'll play along for Jo's sake.

Laura gets up and walks to the fridge. Thank goodness for Island Grocers' prepared foods. She grabs the enchiladas and preheats the oven while George sits at a computer on the island. The wind whistles through the windowpanes, and she hopes dinner will be cooked before the power goes out. She glances over to see what George's doing so intently.

"George!" she screams. "What is that?" Something gray and deeply unfortunate fills the screen.

Eww. She slams the computer shut.

"A geoduck!" he replies delighted, which is somehow worse. He opens the laptop back up.

Laura looks to the sky to give thanks for an ugly sea animal and not something that could land him back in the principal's office. "Please tell me this is for school."

"It is. Can I print this?"

"Let's find a better picture." He is the kid who had a tube of KY jelly taken from him the other day. It's her motherly duty to help him find an image that is a little less suggestive.

"Did you know they grow to be three feet long?" he asks.

Laura snorts despite herself. "I hate that I know that now."

"They're legends of the sea world, Ma. People are obsessed with them."

Laura squints. "Obsessed with that?" First eggplant emojis. Now suggestively shaped sea life.

"Yeppers. They travel from all over the world to see them."

"Really? We have them around here, right?"

"Sure do! They're the treasure of the PNW and ingedinious to Greensea."

"Indigenous," Laura corrects.

Geoducks and housewives. People like the strangest things.

Jo slides back into the kitchen. "Okay. I have some options."

Laura takes the rosé out of the freezer and pours a glass.

"Show me what you've got." At the very least, she's bonding with her daughter.

Jo turns her phone around. A man is mid–finish line, arms raised like he's just conquered Everest.

"This guy's an ultra-runner," Jo says. "And he works in finance."

"I'm not chasing someone through the woods for fun," Laura says. "Next."

Jo swipes. A cowboy, back to the camera, hand on a horse.

"He lives on Greensea?" Laura asks, dumping a bag of salad into a bowl.

"Maybe? It's, like, a twenty-mile radius. Could be mainland."

A ferry commute for a date. Absolutely not.

Laura takes a long sip of wine. "Can't I just take a pottery class and fall in love with someone across the wheel?"

Or better yet, continue accidentally running into a handsome ferry captain and call it fate.

"You want it to feel organic," Meg says.

"Exactly. This feels…" Laura moves her hands around. "Like forced love."

Georgie leaves his laptop and goes to the fridge.

"No more food unless it's an apple! It's almost dinnertime."

"No worries, Ma! I'm getting the crickets out so I can feed Rex."

Rex, the bearded lizard, was a gift for George from Phil when he moved out. The man really knows how to deliver the punches.

Jo shows her another profile. Looks like he's a dad at a baseball game. His child's face has a heart on it.

"He can't be that bad!" Jo's eyes twinkle with possibility.

"How do you even know these are real people? They could be creeps hiding behind AI faces." Laura's sure she heard about a court case like that recently, and it didn't end well.

"Buoy is totally safe. Let's heart this guy," Jo insists.

"What does that mean?" Laura dresses the salad.

"Once you heart him, if he sees your profile and likes you, the app will match you guys."

"I don't know…" Laura hems and haws, just as she hears a gigantic crack and the lights go out. The house groans like it's tired of holding things together.

"Motherf…"

"Don't say it, Ma!" George reprimands as he returns to the fridge.

"Don't open it! Keep all the cold air in."

He nods and walks away as she digs out a flashlight and some candles.

"Oops!" says Jo.

"What's wrong?"

"I'm so sorry!" Jo wraps her arms around Laura.

Meg hovers behind Jo, chewing on a piece of hair.

"What happened?" she asks. Jo does not offer unprompted hugs unless there's a life-threatening emergency.

"I was going to show you first, but then the power went out and it refreshed and—" Jo winces, "—it sent."

"Okay. It's fine. I don't have to respond to him." She sips the rosé and enjoys the liquid swishing down her throat.

"Well, the message was a little flirty and I think it's someone you might see around."

She takes another big sip.

"Who was it?"

"I think it's..." Jo hesitates just long enough, "...Principal Atkins."

"Ma!" George shouts from the other room, feet pounding up the stairs.

Laura closes her eyes.

"I brought Rex's crickets upstairs and the container tipped and now they're everywhere!"

Laura puts her head down on the counter. "Jo," she mumbles. "Can I see your phone?"

Jo hands it over. She looks at the message and the rest of the profile pictures. Laura's stomach sinks. Her throat goes dry. At this rate, George will never graduate from elementary school. Her hands go numb...and then she devises a plan to put the house on the market—crickets and all—in the morning and move far away from this island.

"It's who I think it is, right?" asks Jo.

o mascot! my mascot!

Calder Cunningham

The evening fog wraps around the island, but The Salty Skein glows like a beacon, waiting for the women to converge. Mayor Nickerbottom texted the women to let them know Laverne had the generator going at the shop so the meeting could go on, and that he was tied up with city business due to the storm and would watch Tippy's recording.

God forbid they have to postpone the meeting for a few days. In fairness, part of Calder admires the mayor's persistence. And she knows the women might even be more efficient without his presence.

Laverne Nickerbottom, the mayor's wife, has created a top-notch destination knitting store that puts to rest the adage that knitting is for your grandma. Black walls make the brightly colored skeins of yarn pop. Wicker light fixtures dangle like chandeliers. Boho rugs and a couch filled with quilts call up images of the coffee shop on *Friends*. To top it off, a couple nights a week she hosts a speakeasy in the back with themed drinks and mini sweaters for each cocktail glass. It's hard to believe Laverne Nickerbottom created something so hip, since she still uses a flip phone and thinks TikTok is a new timer app on everyone's phones.

"Greetings," calls Calder as she meanders through the door.

"Hello, sweetheart! I've got the scraps of merino wool all bagged up for you!" Laverne reaches for a bag behind the counter and hands it to Calder.

"I didn't know you knit." Laura strolls in behind Calder.

"Keeps me from doomscrolling," replies Calder. Knitting is an easy way to keep her busy. Calder suffers from the desire to always be doing, and sitting with a knitting project helps her tame that desire. She began by knitting scarves and hats for her kids. Then blankets and sweaters. Since she's knit everything they would possibly accept, she's moved on to knitting dish rags to include in baskets for all her buyers.

Laura takes a seat at the table in the middle of the room. Tippy, already set up in the corner with her dog Bear on her lap, raises two fingers in a hello salute while Laura looks at her phone and types something.

Calder peeks over her shoulder. "Ooh-la-la, a date?"

Laura turns her phone over.

"No, Jo sent a message to someone and I'm trying to make sure he knows it wasn't me. But I can't seem to get into my messages on the app."

"Ahhh, the consequences of letting your children do the work for you."

"I'm not doing that," Laura stumbles. "We were on it together and I had to get up...and then...the power." Laura raises her hand. "It's a long story. And to be honest, being on this app is nothing but trouble. I'm going to take my profile down as soon as the power's back up."

That wouldn't be terrible. Calder's title as the lone Greensea mom on the app could return.

Laverne pops out of the back with a tray of personal charcuterie cups. "We were going to serve Bell's treats in the Greenseasy, but no one's coming out tonight."

Calder admires all the time Bell spends making things beautiful. She loves going into her shop and getting ideas for staging homes. Bell's the first one she calls when she needs any help.

Pine needles fly in, announcing Amanda's arrival. Laverne's running toward her before she can even make it all the way over the threshold.

"Congratulations, dear!" Laverne wraps her arms around Amanda. "This is so exciting!"

"I guess your reaction on the ferry makes sense." Calder chuckles.

"George told me right away," says Laura. "He can't wait to meet the baby."

Amanda nods but doesn't say a word.

"Cat got your tongue?" Calder asks.

"It's all a little overwhelming. I forgot how tired I was during the first trimester."

Laura laughs. "Jo and Meg were Irish twins, and the girls were eight and nine when I had George. It was like starting at the beginning again. I feel your pain!" Laura nibbles a bite of cheese. "Those were pleasant times, when the kids were so little and easily contained. Now they're older, and the world is their oyster, and they're too busy meddling in my life and everyone else's." She pops more cheese in her mouth.

Calder remembers being pregnant with each of her kids like it was yesterday. The cravings for hot and sour soup. The aversion to tomatoes. The last twenty years flew by. If she thinks about it for too long, she'll tear up.

Laura sets her phone down. "Amanda, do you have Principal Atkins's number?"

"Like his personal number?" Amanda practically spits out.

Laura nods. "Just need to touch base with him."

"I have it at home. Remind me and I'll send it to you."

"Tippy, I saw your column," begins Calder.

"Fourth wall!" Tippy huffs.

"The fourth wall is not like pleading the Fifth, Tippy," says Laura.

"I loved how you highlighted the workers in the galley. Great work."

Calder clears her throat before delivering the rest of her thoughts.

"But I resent the fact that you're calling us all housewives in your videos."

"Don't be ridiculous. You know that's only a term people throw around now. I'm not implying you all sit around and eat bonbons while your men bring home the bacon."

"That's exactly what it implies," Calder says.

"Well, that's not how I'm using it. It's a catchphrase. Something to get people's attention. But that's what you want people to think. Oh, these moms are just sitting around not doing anything—and then, surprise! You're all out there killing it."

"I'm not sure that's how everyone sees it. What's the term 'salty mamas' mean?" Laura asks. "I keep hearing people throw it around."

"I asked some people and apparently it's a nickname for moms on Greensea."

"That much I gathered." Laura looks around. "We're all so different. How could one phrase adequately describe all of us?"

"Aren't all nicknames grand over-generalizations?" Tippy asks.

"Well, what does it mean?" Amanda pushes.

"The term 'stay-at-home moms,' or 'housewives,' if you will, has taken on many different iterations. Tradwife, which—you guys are way too messy to be one of those, and plus, none of you have your own sourdough starter, do you?"

Two of them shake their heads. Amanda fiddles with something on her sleeve.

"'Wine moms' is another more en vogue term, albeit a bit problematic when moms use wine to self-soothe while they have young children. Anyway, salty mamas is the local take on wine moms and housewives. Lots of salt air and opinions. You like ferry pours and pretzels. If you ask me, it's cute."

The air in the room stills while the women mull over Tippy's words.

"Sometimes ferry pours and pretzels are the only things keeping me from walking into the tide," Laura admits as she stares into space.

"It's not about having a drink," Amanda says, staring at her hands. "It's about having a few minutes to ourselves where no one needs us."

"Salt air makes us stronger stock and opinions make the island run." Calder clears her throat.

"Still not sure why we need any label at all," says Amanda.

"Because when we have a nickname—working mom, stay-at-home mom, boy mom, girl mom, dance mom—we're seen. We belong to something," says Laura.

Amanda sighs. "It's never enough just to be a mom."

"Try being a woman without kids!" Tippy breaks her own fourth wall.

"Let's get down to business," commands Calder. This conversation could go on for hours if the women are left to ponder their role in society—and the labels that come with it—much longer.

Laura sits up and takes out her notebook. Amanda props her head in her hand.

"After spending the morning in the galley, it's even more obvious that it's a necessary part of the commute," Laura continues. "Personally, I don't think getting rid of something so vital makes any sense."

"We can interrogate the state's numbers for months," Calder says, "or we can raise the money and keep the galley open."

Laura taps her pen. "Let's just get it over with and raise the money."

Amanda and Calder nod in agreement.

"Well, let's start with some ideas. What about an auction?" suggests Calder.

"That's Greensea Elementary's primary fundraising tool. We cannot take the money from the children." Amanda's face stiffens.

"No one ever suggested taking money from the children, dear," says Laura, biting a piece of sausage.

"What about a run?" asks Amanda.

"Great idea!" Calder beats everyone in her age group at the Turkey Trot and the Fourth of July race.

"The Greensea Land Trust does that every year," Laverne adds as she sorts yarn.

"A bake sale," suggests Laura instead.

"Do you bake?" asks Amanda.

Laura rolls her eyes. "Do you run?"

Amanda turns two shades of red. Laura touches her arm in apology.

"We need something that will attract people to the island." Calder tucks a stray hair behind her ear. "In addition, we need to profit off of more people than islanders."

"Do you think we could hijack the pickleball tournament and use that as a fundraiser?" Laura offers.

Pickleball makes Calder's blood boil. Islanders, especially Tippy Meadowcroft, feel such an ownership over it, since it was started here decades ago to keep someone's kids busy. Now, people play it like it's more serious than any Olympic sport. Calder has played it a few times with friends, but each time people mansplained and became aggressive over a sport that they were playing at 1:30 in the afternoon on a Monday. Anyone who has the freedom to be doing that does not have anything to complain about.

"There's no way they'd do that." Calder tsks.

Amanda crosses her arms across her chest before looking at her phone. "Look, can we hurry it up? I have to go and read a chapter of the school read-along to Cleo."

"Can't she read on her own?" pokes Laura.

"Of course, but you realize the point of this whole project is to read together as a family? I take it that's not what you're doing with George?"

Calder appreciates Amanda at her breaking point.

"Okay, that's enough. At this rate we're never going to come up with a plan to raise fifty thousand dollars for the ferry. Might as well start packing your own ferry wine," says Calder.

"The wool festival in Ballard is always popular," Laverne pipes in.

"We need more than knitters." Laura looks around the room.

"The Hood Canal has an oyster fest that's well attended," Amanda adds.

"Oh! Dave would be happy to help with that." Tippy breaks her own fourth wall to promote Dave, who owns Sherman's Shellfish, an oyster farm and seafood shack.

"If another place is doing it, we probably shouldn't bother. We need to be original." Calder strokes the merino yarn in front of her.

"That's it!" Laura exclaims. "George was working on a project for school on geoducks. He said people travel all over to see them."

"Eww, the phallic sea creatures?" Calder asks.

"Yes! I guess they're all the rage," Laura explains.

The women look at each other.

"It's certainly original." Amanda nods her head. "Do you think people would come here to see them?"

"If we made it enough of an event they would." Laura nibbles the last of her charcuterie cup.

"I bet Dave could procure a bunch of them for us," Tippy comments behind the camera.

"How do you eat them?" Calder asks.

"Not sure, but I know people do." Amanda scoots her snacks away from her.

"Oh! Maybe you could have a cooking competition!" Laverne claps her hands. She can't help herself from offering advice.

"Certainly not doing a dessert dash after the last fiasco." Calder will never let the women forget the battle that ensued over a dessert at Applehill Farm's Apple Festival.

"Greensea Geoduck Festival...it kind of has a ring to it," Amanda says.

Calder isn't sold. Geoducks are messy and slimy. Festivals are loud. They draw crowds who drink beer from plastic cups and don't know how to recycle. Not the kind of people who linger, pop in at a showing, and ask about school districts.

"A geoduck festival!" Laverne claps her hands. "That's the best idea I've heard in decades."

Calder grabs her phone and types in 'geoduck' and starts to read what she finds out loud. "The longest living animals. They live to be a hundred and forty years old! Can we ethically support killing them to celebrate?" She's grasping at straws, but if she's going to turn this tide, that's what she has to do.

Laura shrugs. "Do they provide any benefits? Like if we let them live, do they do anything for us?"

Calder scans her phone and shifts her weight. "I don't think so."

"Then who cares?" Amanda points out.

A hush falls over the women.

"A festival is a lot of work for the three of us to take on," mentions Calder. Maybe she can find some donors to cover the $50,000. "We all have a lot going on." She looks right toward Amanda. "Especially our volunteer extraordinaire."

Amanda blushes.

Laverne laughs. "I bet if the three of you sketched out what you needed done, Barb, Bell, and I could do all the legwork."

Barb Sherman, Bell Meadowcroft, and Laverne Nickerbottom are the older version of the committee gathered at the table.

"That wouldn't be fair to ask you to do that," Calder says, already mentally listing the logistics she wouldn't have to control.

Amanda straightens. "We're not asking them. Laverne suggested it."

"Exactly!" Laverne laughs again. "It may be our elder era, but you know we are happy to help out as much as we can."

"What if we broke it down into three parts and each of you worked with one of us?" Amanda offers.

"Brilliant," Laura says.

Calder nods, even as a familiar tightening settles in her chest. Three teams. Too many moving parts. And a mascot made of slime. So many things could go wrong.

boy or girl

Amanda Willows

"Let's make a deal," says Cleo, clearly aware Amanda's teetering on the edge. "I'll read this chapter if we can charge my iPad in the car when I'm done."

The untimely power outage last night canceled school, and now Amanda is trying to convince Cleo to read *Because of Winn-Dixie*. To top it all off, her stomach is still on the fritz, and she can't watch her reality TV shows while she eats Saltines. Although it seems her own life is becoming enough of a show on its own.

If only Thomas had agreed to her insistent pleas to get a small generator so they could still have the fridge and one outlet during the recurring, incessant power outages that plague Greensea. Then she wouldn't be contemplating sitting in the parking lot of Island Grocers, looking for viable internet reception so she and her precious kiddo could spend a quiet thirty minutes on their devices. But he insisted a generator wasn't in their budget and not using electricity from time to time would actually help them out. He certainly won't change his mind now.

"Deal," Amanda blurts, and runs to the bathroom.

Cleo seems to have mastered the art of speed reading when Amanda returns and passes her quick quiz on the chapter, so they set out for the parking lot.

The sky's a piercing blue this morning with a few clouds on the horizon. Phew. The storm is on its way out of here. The driveway is filled with pine needles scattered like confetti from a birthday party. Branches litter the roads, but there's nothing major as far as Amanda can see, which leads her to believe the power will be restored sooner rather than later.

Greensea moms have all had the same idea for entertaining their children, as Island Grocers' parking lot is packed. Amanda can only find a compact parking spot, but the minivan can squeeze into it, especially since she has no plans to use the doors. Cleo puts on her headphones and dawdles on her device while Amanda's phone pings with text messages that are finally able to go through.

Soccer practice is still on.

Milk delivery will be late.

And a reminder from Laura Prescott that she wants Principal Atkins's home phone number.

Amanda was so tired after she got home last night, she didn't even think about Laura's request again. What did little Georgie do now? Cheat on the weekly spelling test? Free the class gerbil? Knock the power out to the whole island? Tongues will wag. How does that child end up at the center of all the action? With two highly educated parents you'd think he'd be out of the limelight. She shares the contact information and makes a mental note to dig around and see if she can figure out what's going on.

"Ahhh!" A guttural scream escapes her mouth as a face appears in the window of her van. Amanda grabs her stomach—

her maternal instincts kicking in for the lima bean. She rolls down her window to lodge a complaint.

"You scared the crap out of me, Mayor!"

Mayor Nickerbottom and his gray beard stare back at her.

"Mom, you said crap," squeaks a voice from the backseat. How'd she even hear that with her headphones on?

"I've fast-tracked the Geoduck Festival permit at the city. Brilliant idea! Just brilliant." The mayor kisses his fingers and throws the kiss to the sky.

"Is that why you scared the bejeezus out of me?"

"No! No! Sorry! Ms. Willows, we're going to need your help." The mayor's eyebrows have a meeting at the bridge of his nose.

"I'm already helping with the ferry committee. We met at The Salty Skein last night as promised," she says. How quickly he's forgotten.

"No, no, not with that. You know the Willard farm provides lunch for the kids. Their generator conked out this morning, and they need to get the yogurt parfaits for tomorrow's school lunch refrigerated within the next hour, or the kids will not have their organic, small-batch, locally-sourced, hand-stirred yogurt parfaits topped with free-range blueberries and artisanal granola!"

Her first reaction is not one she's familiar with—she wants to tell Mayor Nickerbottom to buy the kids some Oreos and call it a day. She shakes her head and wills the egregious thoughts away—no child, or person, should be consuming high-fructose corn syrup. Pushing the hankering for a sweet treat aside, she thinks for a moment and comes up with a plan.

"Will the power be restored soon?" she asks.

The mayor deflates like a juice pouch drained by a three-year-old. "Nope." He rubs his brow. "You haven't heard?"

"In case you haven't noticed, information is a little slow moving this morning. I'm just beginning to go through all my texts and emails." It's almost as if Greensea should go back to the old days, when news traveled around the island via bulletin board and islanders didn't rely on electronic messages.

"We're hosed. It's a complete disaster." His shoulders slump. "The Carpenter couple was having a backyard gender reveal during the windstorm. Reagan's mom had decorated the backyard with blue and pink balloons."

Amanda gasps. Greensea is a balloon-free island. What were they thinking?

"The balloons flew away in the wind, got tangled around our major transformer on the north end, caused an insulation fire, and melted several components—taking the whole grid down. The electricians are on it, but it will be a while. Until then, I'm working with the city council to ensure nothing like this happens again."

Nothing says "parenting readiness" like crippling the whole island with your balloon-fueled ego.

"Girl or boy?" she asks.

"They're too embarrassed to reveal."

Hmmph. Of course they are. But back to the task at hand.

"Does Island Grocers have a generator?"

"Of course they do!" His eyes practically roll out of their sockets.

"Go inside and talk to them about making space for the parfaits while I get some of the moms in the parking lot to stop scrolling Instagram and follow me to the farm. We'll pick up the concoctions and deliver them to the store."

"Bless you, Amanda Willows. What would this community do without your quick mind and good heart?"

Her thoughts exactly. If only her dedicated volunteerism came with a paycheck. She hates that she loves being the one people call in a crisis. Maybe that's her problem—she mistakes exhaustion for purpose.

She takes an antacid from her purse and scans the parking

lot. She scooches out of her tight parking spot and recruits three other moms in minivans to help, and in exchange promise to take all the kids to the playground after they've re-homed the parfaits.

Hours later, as Amanda sits on a swing and watches the kids run around, she opens her Notes app and titles a list: *Geoduck Festival: Things That Can Go Wrong.*

First bullet: *Power. No balloons!*

greensea gazette

Dear Islanders,

We can usually blame Mother Nature and the gale-force winds she sends up the Strait of Juan de Fuca for any power outages, but not this week! We can place the blame fully where it rests—ignorance and big egos. Who likes gender reveals anyway? But all's well that ends well...sort of. Mayor Nickerbottom is working with everyone's least favorite online delivery company to see if they will stop selling balloons to islanders. Not the first thing we'd ask that company to stop selling, but oh, well. We doubt he'll get it done, but it's worth a try!

Yes, you heard it right! Greensea is hosting the first annual Geoduck (pronounced gooey duck—think slime) Festival. Keep your comments clean and to yourself. We know how spring festivals work around here, so get out your rain boots and slickers and start praying to whatever weather god you believe in. The time-frame is tight, but we all know whatever the housewives (a.k.a. Salty Mamas) set their minds to gets done. And hell hath no fury like a woman facing pushback for trying to get something done on this island. Lest we forget what happened when the city council tried to stop the plastic gnomes from popping up all over the place— they expanded like sea monkeys overnight. Imagine the kind of energy the housewives are going to bring to the festival. Buckle your seatbelts, Greensea! Game on!

xoxo,
GG

the universe knows best

Laura Prescott

Laura looks at the yellow legal pad in front of her, titled *Geoduck Festival Final*. It's filled with cross-outs and arrows. And three question marks next to food safety. She's divided up the list of tasks, crossed out the word *final* in exchange for *v1*, and she's attempting to put it in a spreadsheet when Becky runs into Laura's office.

"Have you seen it yet?"

"No, what?" Laura's afraid to know what she's talking about now.

"The latest housewives video." Becky thrusts her phone into Laura's hands.

Laura clocks the view count in the bottom left corner before she clocks herself. It's climbing. For better or worse.

It begins with a photo of Laura and the bio Tippy's created, and continues with a mash-up of the moment Laura exploded the milk, the captain wiping it off the brim of her hat, and then the cereal incident at Island Grocers. Laura watches as she sees the two of them kneeling in the aisle together. The video concludes with Laura watching him walk off. The kneeling shot lingers longer than it should. Laura has no memory of staying there that long, but the edit proves otherwise.

She watches herself shake his hand and smile at him, and is almost betrayed by her own face.

The screen goes black and reads, "Who needs a dating app when there's a hot ferry captain?"

This isn't just footage—it's a story. And she didn't approve the narrative.

Laura hands the phone back to Becky. She didn't even notice Tippy in the store. Are there video vigilantes filming for her?

"This is so much more than I signed up for," Laura laments.

"It's adorable, though." Becky's in her late twenties. "You look great and your meet-cute is top notch."

"Meet-cute?" Laura's not familiar with the term Becky used like she was pulling it out of a law dictionary.

"Yeah. You know, the moment the two lead characters have a run-in, and it leads to the beginning of their romance."

A romantic relationship? He simply turned up when she needed a hand. "I don't know if that's a meet-cute or simply two random incidents where he helped me clean up a mess."

Becky laughs. "Lean into it. You met, and it was cute."

Laura lifts a corner of her mouth as Becky returns to her desk.

Laura's brain fills with thoughts. The privacy she claimed to love and was mad at Jo for violating is being violated on the regular by Tippy.

But Laura agreed to allow that to happen.

She pulls the video up on her phone and watches it again. She takes in everything he has in his basket—frozen lasagna, bread, a bag of salad, and a container of chocolate milk. Chocolate milk? Is that his? He must be young at heart.

There's no doubt he's handsome—his eyelashes must reach

the dock before the ferry. But what's she supposed to do about it? Stalk him on the boat and ask him out? Not likely.

She puts her phone down, looks at her geoduck spreadsheet, and pops open her email. She begins a letter to the committee about the continued scope of filming, using phrases like *clarity, consent, expectations*, and *moving forward*. She sighs again and returns to the video, this time focusing on the comments.

```
Laura's great revenge!
Another salty mama bites the dust.
The captain is always near the drama.
```

All of the sudden, Laura's mind turns to the captain. Did he give consent to be filmed or has Tippy violated his rights? She sticks the email she was writing into drafts and blasts out another to Tippy, ensuring she's taken his rights into consideration. This could affect his job. Or his life. Maybe he's married. *Oh my gosh!* What if he's married and people think they're having an affair? Chocolate milk and a salad imply food groups and a family.

Laura's phone pings with a text.

Tippy: Chill out. The captain signed a release.

Laura taps the pen in her hand even faster. He agreed to the video. Before or after he saw what Tippy put together? The thoughts in her head move around like a disjointed legal brief. Laura does not like things that are out of her control. She likes rules and standards. This has none of that.

"You okay in there?" Becky calls in.

Laura realizes she's drumming her fingers, too.

"Yep. Yep. All good."

She flushes it all from her mind and returns to her geoduck spreadsheet. With the same energy she was using to tap her desk, she creates a list of to-dos and assigns names to them. Food? Covered. Activities? Done. Legal formalities? Double done. PR campaign? She doesn't even want to touch that, but inputs a list of what she considers to be appropriate ways to advertise.

Tonight's Phil's night with the kids. Laura always busies herself with some kind of work in an attempt to forget her situation. Right now, the geoduck festival is the lucky recipient of her frenetic energy.

After a couple more hours, she plods home. It always makes her stop short when her house is quiet. Her heart and mind automatically think something's wrong. And it is. It isn't right that her marriage ended and her kids are forced to spend one night a week with Phil.

After a piece of toast, she curls up with a glass of rosé in bed and watches the video one more time, knowing that if this were a tape in a VCR, she would have worn it out. She can't help but look at the comments again.

```
Look at the way she's watching him.
Laura has a heart.
```

When people talk about Laura, it's usually her competence in the courtroom. Here they're discussing the merits of her emotions. It's an entirely different ballgame, and one she has no control over—no matter what Tippy's spin on it is.

Her phone pings.

> Jo: Is that organic enough for you?

Hmmph. The universe did hand her exactly what she was looking for.

greensea blows

Tippy Meadowcroft

Tippy hops on Bertha and pedals over to The Reformation—another repurposed church, only this one's a Pilates studio. The Reformation has twelve reformers—exercise equipment resembling medieval torture devices—lined up and waiting for the lucky class participants. Tippy alternates between a 9 a.m. class with women who stay at home and today's early-bird special at 6, filled with those who head to the office or need to get a workout in before kids get up.

Tippy strides over to her favorite reformer. She likes the way the morning light shines through the old stained-glass windows at this machine. It's in front of a mirror, but not too close to the dreaded altar that gives her the creeps. Close enough to the bathroom if she needs it and close enough to the holy-water-font-turned-water-cooler. And the best part is her spot centers her within the sanctuary—ready to glean any tidbits that may or may not make their way into GG's next column.

Tippy rolls her neck to the side, catching the glare of the person next to her—Laura.

"Martha won't let you film in here, will she?" Laura's eyes narrow.

"I'm off the Housewives clock for the next hour." Tippy adjusts her straps.

"Can you take me off the clock for good?" Laura asks.

"That video was gold. If you don't land that Ferry McSwoony dude after this, there's no hope for you."

"McSwoony? I thought his name was McHottyPants."

Tippy cackles. "That's even better, Laura. I knew you two were a match made in heaven."

If she's honest, Tippy had no idea they'd create magic on the screen—but judging from the number of views the piece got, lots of people want to see their chemistry.

"Welcome to the church of Pilates. Get ready to pray at our altar," says Martha. Her irreverent start to every class cues Tippy to take a deep breath and prepare to throw everything out of her mind for the next fifty-five minutes.

"Let's begin on three heavy springs with your heels on the foot bar. Exhale as you push out. Inhale when you come in." Martha paces down the aisle of reformers.

"You know I'm a lawyer, right?" Laura spits out in a heavy whisper as they bend their legs back in.

"So?" Tippy answers during her exhale.

"You made me look like a floozy! The opposing counsel might see that. Or the judge!"

"And lift your feet up and put your arches on the foot bar in second position. Out and in," Martha commands.

"I didn't make you look like anything. I simply recorded you, which you agreed to!" The top of Tippy's foot slips off the foot bar, forcing her to reposition herself.

"Let's all focus on our footwork." Martha hovers between their reformers with the gentle reminder.

"Come in on an inhale, sit up using your core, and come

down to two red springs. Lie back down and take the straps in your hands." Martha's voice echoes through the space.

"You turned my potential dating life into entertainment." Laura puts her feet in the straps.

"Concentrate, Laura, we're doing supine arms." Martha's stern voice has arrived.

Tippy shakes her head and gives a little snort. "People love seeing you look alive."

"Arms up, legs at forty-five degrees, frog in when you pull your arms."

Tippy's carriage slams.

"Control the close, Tip." Martha's not leaving their area.

"What you're doing is beyond the scope of the agreement."

This time Laura's reformer slams as she comes in.

"Eenouggh, you two!" Martha implores.

A hush falls over the room, and Tippy and Laura move through the remainder of the class in silence.

When the church bell rings and class ends, Laura rushes for the door.

"You don't get to decide who I am on this island." She yanks her jacket from the hook.

"I didn't. People already decided. I just filmed it," Tippy snipes back before Laura disappears out the door.

———

Tippy rides Bertha down to the smoothie truck behind Island Grocers to order her Greensea Delight—a kale, spinach, pineapple, and banana smoothie. She sits at the picnic table next to the truck.

The air has a nip, but it's a great spot to people-watch. A lot happens in the parking lot of Island Grocers, and the pavement never lies. People show their worst selves in between the white lines. Mad dashes for last-minute ingredients and road rage incidents take precedence. Today the most exciting thing is the Flanders' nanny pulling in in an oversized Suburban. Wails echo through the lot when she opens the door and gets out of the car. In the blink of an eye, she runs in and buys several large containers of goldfish crackers, then returns to the car.

Ahhh! The Flanders must have been in charge of snack today. Annoying, but that's nothing to write about.

Tippy collects her smoothie from the counter and returns to the table to check her email. The GG anonymous tip box is filled with possible balloon violations. Boring. A complaint about pickleball taking over even more tennis courts. Nothing new there. Completely overdone. And a possible wife-swapping incident. Hmmm. Possible storyline. *Will have to explore that one.*

She scrolls down further and sees an email from a company called Blow Bar. She opens it and reads it quickly while she sucks on her smoothie.

What? A sponsorship opportunity? Is this real?

She hovers her finger over the email address. It looks legit.

Dear Ms. Meadowcroft,

In advance of the opening of our Greensea location, we would love to partner with the *Housewives* by providing fresh blowouts for the women and sponsoring an upcoming episode. We think it's a natural fit to celebrate local businesses while helping everyone look their best on camera, and we'd be excited to collaborate on ways to feature the partnership in a fun and authentic way.

Please let us know if this is something you'd be interested in discussing further. We'd be happy to share additional details and explore how we can make this a great fit for everyone.

Sincerely,

Bronwyn Madderstock

Blow Bar? Is that a chain? Surely Greensea Island isn't

allowing a chain to come to the island. Tippy searches for the company in her browser. Blow Bar appears with the web address of www.greenseablows.com. Tippy throws her head back and lets out a guffaw.

"Greensea Blows!" she says to no one. Genius. It's the perfect title for their next *Housewives* episode.

The website looks real, and it seems to be a one-of-a-kind salon that may mimic a franchise. Tippy searches Bronwyn's name. Interesting. Looks like she lives in Seattle. How did this slip by Tippy? First the closing of the galley and now this. Is she no longer any good at her job? No; she shakes her head. Tippy Meadowcroft is not behind. She's ahead, and can be the one to help announce Blow Bar to the island.

Tippy sends a quick response indicating she'd love more details.

A sponsor. Already. Filming the women may be the best idea she's had yet. A sponsor means legitimacy. And legitimacy means Tippy has a real role in this whole thing.

famous last words

Calder Cunningham

Calder begins every morning in front of her laptop with a cup of hot water and lemon. Today the lemon bites the back of her throat as she sees a spreadsheet from Laura. It's not even 9 a.m.

Holy shit, Laura, do you sleep?

The entire gross sea creature festival is outlined and color-coded, with tasks assigned to each of them. Seeing it all in writing means they're really putting on this godforsaken event. For someone who claimed she didn't have enough time to work on it, Laura sure has found some. The spreadsheet is clearly laid out and removes most of the thinking from what Calder will need to do. At least that's one clear benefit.

Judging from all the work on the festival and the release of the meet-cute video, Laura should be off Buoy by now. No need to look for love when she's found it in the cereal aisle. She's been a busy bee in all the ways.

Calder clicks over to Buoy. A little red dot indicates she has a message. When she clicks on it, a message from GreenseaPhil123 pops up.

`Would you like to meet?`

For the last few weeks, she's been exchanging messages with this user. They're compatible via a screen, and he says he's an island local. Calder's done her best to dig up info on the username, to little avail. Messaging is safe, but meeting him is not messaging. Messaging disappears, but meeting waves at you while you're walking on the ferry. And waves start island rumors, which ferment faster than kombucha. But if she wants to find someone to take up space with her in her too-big home, she's going to have to take the next step.

Calder starts to pace around the kitchen counter. She circles her ninety-six-inch matte black soapstone gourmet island twice before realizing she's wearing a groove into her morning.

She can't meet Mr. 123 at Codmother's or The Old Owl. Everyone would see her there.

She texts Fern to see if she has any idea.

> Fern: That's a little cringe to ask your
> daughter where to go on a date.

Of course. There is always a 50/50 chance whatever Calder asks Fern will elicit that type of response. But it was worth the risk, since she's never sure what will lead to a positive mother-daughter conversation.

> Fern: Also proud of you for dating again. But
> still cringe.

Calder screenshots the text as Mr. Darcy lingers near her feet, waiting for his morning treat. Her phone pings once more.

> Fern: Do an activity. Paint pottery. Ax
> throwing. Kayak lessons. It's less focus on
> you as a couple but still lets you get to
> know him.

Bingo! That's a perfect idea. Calder thinks about all the

activities on the island. Horseback riding, but she hates horses. Hiking? If he's a serial killer, the woods aren't ideal for her. Calder scans her brain to remember what the kids did when they were home. Fern spent all her time playing lacrosse, and Fitz did all things theater and dance.

Hmmm.

Dancing.

Maybe she could set up a private lesson at Miss Kitty's dance studio. It's secluded. She's sure she could rent it. And if all goes well, maybe they could pop over to the Greenseasy at The Salty Skein. Laverne keeps everything that happens there on the down low.

With renewed interest, Calder texts Miss Kitty to put her plan in motion.

Calder: Think dirty dancing vibes

This will be perfect.

Miss Kitty texts back with a thumbs up.

Next step is replying to GreenseaPhil123 to invite him to the studio tomorrow evening. Calder throws caution to the wind, storing her common sense away.

Let's spend a night moving to our own beat.

Within thirty seconds he replies.

I'd love to cha cha with you.

Corny, but she catches a giggle in her throat. She reads it again. Then one more time, slower. Her giggle turns into butterflies.

Calder sprints to her closet. She has a dress that's pale pink and tea length. She bought it for a fundraiser years ago. A different life. A different version of herself, who hadn't yet learned how to fold disappointment into polite conversation. Perfect. She looks at her nails. Shit. She dials Glenda at Greensea Glam.

"Glenda, it's Calder. I have a 911. Can you fit me in today?"

"For you, of course. Can you be here in fifteen?"

"You bet."

Calder throws on a barn jacket, tucks her hair into a neat bun, and jumps into her car. Greensea Glam is the island's all-organic nail salon. Glenda makes her own non-toxic nail polishes filled with seasonal colors. The Big Dark—charcoal grey. Luck o' the Island—minty green. Today Calder's going to go for 7:05 Ferry—a barely-there pink.

"A geoduck festival, Calder?" Glenda asks as she files Calder's nails.

"Upscale geoduck. Think Coachella, but add shellfish." Calder can usually sell anything, but she's having a hard time even selling this idea to herself. Maybe if she involves Hunter Sorenson—Greensea's local five-star chef—he can bring a touch of gourmet to the day. The Claw is an upscale restaurant even while featuring sea creatures. He's got to have some advice. Heck, they might even be able to use him in some publicity for the festival, which would bring a different level of clientele.

"You're not going to have a mascot, are you?" Glenda moves onto Calder's other hand.

Calder shivers. She hopes no one plans to dress up like a geoduck. People would be tossing their cookies before they even arrived at the festival.

"If anyone suggests plush merchandise," Glenda says, "I'm calling the health department. And the festival logo? How are you going to do that without making it X-rated?"

Another good point that Laura didn't address on her spreadsheet. Mayor Nickerbottom should have put Glenda on the committee. She's full of ideas.

"And please, remember to tell everyone not to put googly eyes on any of the images." Glenda sighs. "Enough about the festival. An emergency appointment is not very Calder. What gives?"

Calder swallows a breath and leans in. "I have a date."

Glenda drops Calder's hands and claps the nail table. Calder gives a quick glance to her left and her right to see if she knows anyone else in the salon.

"Calder Cunningham! That is the best news I've heard in a long time." Glenda blows a bubble with her gum. "This manicure is on the house."

"No, I couldn't. I won't." Calder shakes her head. After her ex's messy affairs, everyone on Greensea would be happy to see her find a second chance at love.

"Need any other services while you're here? A little wax?" Glenda winks.

Calder raises her eyebrows. Waxing? Should she? It's only a first date. There's no way things will end up down there.

"No, no. That's not necessary."

"Famous last words," says Glenda.

double trouble

Amanda Willows

Amanda scooches on the paper cover on the ultrasound table.

"I don't know. I might have miscarried. I've been really crampy and just don't feel right."

The tech nods. Thomas squirms in the plastic chair. If he moves again and ignores her glares, Amanda may ask him to leave the exam room.

"Okay," says the tech. "Let's see what we can find."

She squirts the cold jelly on Amanda's stomach without even warning her it will be cold. Yes, she is a nurse and knows that—but still, common decency! She turns the screen to the side so Amanda can't see it and pushes the probe on her stomach.

"You think you're about ten weeks?"

"I think so. Honestly, I'm not a hundred percent sure about anything. I've been really busy lately and haven't been tracking my cycle at all." Between Cleo's life and volunteer stuff at school, she's honestly not sure when her last period was. It has been ten weeks since Cleo was at the sleepover, but there were other times before and after. Still, only that one stands out.

The tech probes around and then turns a knob on the machine.

"Listen," she says, and the sound of a heartbeat fills the room.

"It's fine!" Amanda presses a palm to her heart. Everything has been so public that she couldn't imagine going through a public miscarriage, too. A baby. It's true. It's actually going to happen.

"They're fine," the tech says.

"They?" asks Thomas in the corner.

Amanda stares at the tech.

"Yes! Twins!" She turns the screen towards Amanda and Thomas so they can see the little jelly bean-looking things—two of them.

Twins. Two babies. Not one surprise. But two. Amanda's head fills with things they'll need. Two cribs. Two strollers. Two high chairs. And then there will be two teenagers. Two cars. Two college payments. She pulls herself back into this moment. "But —but—why am I cramping? Does everything look okay?"

"Yes, your uterus is expanding at a faster rate than with a single pregnancy. That explains why you're feeling this way."

Thomas makes a choking sound in the corner. Amanda gives him another death stare.

"Will you stop!" she commands.

"We're having two babies? At the same time?" Thomas gasps out.

"Yes! That's what twins are!" She looks at him again. His shoulders are moving up and down as if he's developed a twitch.

"What's wrong with you?" She's trying to be excited in the moment, and he's sucking all the joy out of the room. They are a young and healthy family. They are well suited to give these babies a fantastic life.

"We have one kid and now we're going to have three." He does the math on his fingers.

"Good job, Thomas. You can do first grade math."

Seriously. She has no idea what's going on with him. Is he having a stroke?

The tech takes a few measurements on the screen.

"You're right. You're ten weeks. Your doctor will sit down with you and go through everything else at your appointment."

The tech leaves, giving Amanda a chance to figure out what's going on with Thomas.

"What's up?" she asks Thomas.

"Amanda, we'll need to make some changes."

"What do you mean?"

"Kids are expensive. You know how much Cleo costs. Multiply that by two more and I'm not sure I make enough money."

Her head starts swirling. What's she supposed to do? She has nine months to figure out how to make this work.

The doctor comes in and goes through everything with them. Words float in and out of Amanda's head. High risk. Will be important to get to the hospital in time. Ferry. Blah blah blah.

A nurse comes in and leads her to the lab. After the blood-work is done, she can finally breathe.

"Thomas, this is a good thing." She forces a smile, tucking both their worries away.

He draws in a deep breath and reaches for her hand. "I know it is. But we're not getting bonuses. So we'll need to figure some-thing out."

Amanda's whole body clenches. She's going to have to go back to the clinic. The thought of germs and being on her feet all day makes her stomach turn—especially now, pregnant with twins. There has to be an option that doesn't involve seeing patients.

She slips her hand from his and shifts into problem-solving mode. She'll text the clinic, see what's possible. Maybe prescription calls, patient callbacks from home. A few hours a week is better than nothing.

A noise in the distance gets their attention. A redhead. Standing next to a bike.

"Tippy! What are you doing in the parking lot of the doctor's office?" asks Thomas, shielding his face from her camera.

Amanda squints and purses her lips together.

"How's everything going, Amanda?" Tippy asks.

"Fine. Just fine."

"Get any news?"

Amanda realizes she's still holding the pictures from the ultrasound. Tippy zooms in on the pieces of paper.

"Wait! Does that say twin A and twin B?"

Amanda pulls them close to her chest—picture side down.

"This is gold!" Tippy cheers. "You three women are a gift that keeps giving! They're going to love this!"

"Who's going to love it?"

"Our new sponsor!"

Sponsor? Wait a second. Someone is willing to pay Tippy for the *Housewives* content. Wheels turn in Amanda's head. Could this be the break she needs? Could the housewife content help her family too?

Amanda turns toward Thomas. "You can get to the ferry on your own, right?"

He looks down the street. It's a half a mile walk, but it's all downhill. Thomas shrugs. "I guess so?"

"Good. I need to speak with Tippy." Amanda doesn't want Thomas hanging around for their conversation. His opinion is unpredictable, and she might need to soften the truth before she shares it.

Thomas leans in for a kiss. Amanda offers him a cheek.

"We'll make this work, somehow," he whispers in her ear.

Amanda and Tippy watch Thomas leave the parking lot and walk toward the terminal.

"Tell me about the sponsors."

"Only one so far! But a salon has offered blowouts to all of you and a decent sum to sponsor an episode."

"They want to do our hair?" Amanda never has her hair done. She trims her stick-straight hair on her own. At least Thomas can't accuse her of wasting money. She wonders if anybody would even be able to do anything special with her hair.

"And what are you going to do with the money?"

Tippy takes a deep breath. "I haven't figured that out yet. It seems obvious that we add it to the galley fund, but who knows —we may raise enough through the festival."

"Have any other companies been in touch?"

"Not yet. But I imagine it's only a matter of time once they see we have one sponsor."

Saving the money for the galley fund is the right choice, but it's only fair that they each keep any products they might get. And babies, especially twins, need a ton of things that cost money.

"Has every video been getting the same amount of traffic?"

Tippy rubs her hands together. "It started out slow, but we've been gaining traction with your pregnancy story."

Of course. Who doesn't love a good medical drama caught on camera? Amanda figures if it's happening—with or without her—she might as well use it to her advantage.

"And then the meet-cute episode took it to the next level."

Amanda's news. The twins. That should be a banger.

"What are your plans?" Amanda's heartbeat climbs.

"What do you mean?"

"I know you pitched the producers about a show. Are you trying to get this on the air?"

Tippy's gaze drifts away. "No. Right now I'm going small. I want to build the brand and then let people come to us."

"Okay."

"Okay?" Tippy cocks her head to the side.

"I'm in," Amanda says.

"I know you're in. You signed the papers."

"No, I want to help you build the brand."

Tippy turns her head and takes in their surroundings. She turns to Amanda and nods.

"I could use an assistant." Tippy holds out her hand and Amanda shakes, sealing the deal.

"So what's our first step?"

"We need more footage of all of you, like what I got of you coming out the doctor's office today. We have to film more than the meetings."

"Well, I'm happy to help you with that effort!"

Amanda looks at her watch.

"I've got to go," says Amanda. "I need to take Cleo to dance."

"Okay." Tippy wraps her in a hug. "This is going to be amazing!"

Amanda smiles as the minivan putters over to pick up Cleo. She cracks her window and turns up the music. Maybe all her dedicated volunteer work will pay off in real money after all. She'd love to show Thomas she can do it all—her way.

As soon as Cleo jumps in the car, Amanda hands her a container of pre-cut veggies and dip.

"I've got some pretty big news," Amanda says.

Cleo munches on a carrot. "Yeah?"

"I'm having twins!"

"Two babies? At the same time?" Cleo sits up, stretching the limits of her seatbelt.

"Yep!"

"What if we get them mixed up?" Cleo asks. Horror fills Amanda's mind before she remembers the doctor said they're fraternal and not identical. They will have differences.

"We'll paint one of their toes!" Amanda doesn't feel like getting into the nuts and bolts of twin babies as they pull up to dance class.

"Hey, Miss Kitty," says Amanda to Cleo's impossibly chic dance teacher.

"We're having twins!" Cleo announces to the entire room filled with moms and kids.

"Coooonnnngratulations, daaaarling," Miss Kitty purrs.

"Thanks!" Amanda blushes.

Miss Kitty's holding a box of pokers with fur tips. "What are you doing with those?"

"Setting up for a private dance lesson with one of your compadres and her date."

"My friend?" Amanda wonders who Miss Kitty would consider her friend. Amanda knows a lot of people, most people on the island, but would consider very few of them her friends.

"Calder."

Amanda's head swirls. Calder on a date. She must text Tippy. That's the perfect thing for them to get next. No, wait. This may be breaking a confidence. She rubs her stomach and shakes her head. If Calder wanted it to be private, she wouldn't have picked a dance studio. Her phone's in her hand before she finishes the thought.

———

With her growing stomach and to-do list, Amanda hops into bed. Thomas is snoring already, as he came up an hour ago while she checked off a few more tasks on Laura's spreadsheet. Laura tasked Amanda with creating a kid area and finding volunteers for the day—things Amanda could do in her sleep.

Amanda can't help but watch Tippy's video again after she climbs under the covers, pulling the duvet over her head so the light doesn't bother Thomas. A compilation of all Amanda's moments thus far—fainting, feeling sick, the test, and now she's added the ultrasound picture—it ends with the words *Double Happiness.* She remembers a card from her great-aunt with that phrase when she and Thomas got married. She vaguely remembers the Japanese characters. She searches the Internet and finds it quickly...extra good luck. Maybe things are working out like they're supposed to. And maybe, just maybe, her little family of five will handle it beautifully.

dirty dancing

Calder Cunningham

Calder checks herself in the mirror before she leaves. What good fortune to have her hair blown out today. Of course, Tippy had no idea why Calder volunteered for the first available appointment. Her chestnut curls frame her face perfectly.

She can't help but wonder if the pale pink dress with nude heels has seen better days. Setting up a blind date at Miss Kitty's dance studio is a bold move, even for her. But if she doesn't take a risk now, her future is clear—takeout, reruns, and no one touching her but the cat. She turns her head from side to side. A little extra plum color on her cheeks is what she needs. She runs back upstairs to her bathroom and applies it under the glow of her mirrors.

Please don't let this man be a creep. The warm touch of another human sounds so delightful, Calder worries she'll lower her standards for someone, anyone, who shows her attention. She tucks her resolve into her purse and reviews her plan. Lesson with Miss Kitty—and if all goes well, a drink at the Greenseasy.

She's kept the last part to herself in case he gives her the ick and she decides to abort before the drink.

"Wish me luck, Mr. Darcy," Calder says as she closes the front door.

Rather than her steamy audiobook, Calder opts for her hype music, as Fern calls it. A playlist the kids made during the darkest days of the divorce, equal parts love and encouragement. Now it makes her smile every time she hears it, pulling her somewhere between gratitude and the undeniable urge to sing along.

Calder sucks in a breath before she opens the door to the studio. It's a familiar and comfortable spot, as her son Fitz danced with Miss Kitty for many years. The studio, a renovated boat repair shop, is big and airy. A barre and mirror line one side of the room opposite the floor-to-ceiling windows. The rest of the space is open. The only modern touch is the top-tier stereo system in the corner. As she opens the door, she sees that the place has been transformed tonight into something out of a movie, causing Calder to gasp.

Long red velvet curtains are drawn in front of the windows. The exposed brick walls hold candelabras with—she sniffs. Are those vanilla candles? Mardi Gras masks dangle from the pillars, up-lit with red lights. Matching rose petals sit on the floor. Calder looks toward the bistro table set up in the corner and sees a bevy of whips and handcuffs on the table, ready for Calder and her date. She clutches her pearls. What the hell!

Miss Kitty and her husband, Kit, saunter out from the back room and stand in front of the set-up like proud parents.

She takes another step into the room and releases her necklace. "Oh. My. God. What have you done?"

Miss Kitty and Kit toggle their heads, admiring the set-up. "Just what you asked for, my dear," Miss Kitty says, the way someone explains a murder weapon.

Miss Kitty reaches for her phone in her pocket, pulls on the readers that dangle around her neck, and reads her text aloud.

"'Think dirty dancing.' I thought the elegant vibes would be more suitable than something from a strip club."

"I wanted *Dirty Dancing* with campy vibes and the lift at the end, not *Fifty Shades*!"

Miss Kitty slides her readers off. "But, my dear, you didn't capitalize the letter 'D' in either word, so I didn't know you were referring to the movie."

Calder runs a hand over her hair. "There's not enough time to do anything about it now. Do you think you can shove the whips and the handcuffs in the closet before he arrives?"

As if on cue, the door opens. Calder turns around and drops her beaded clutch to the ground as Kit moves swiftly to hide the props.

"What are YOU doing here?" Calder rubs her hands down her pink dress as if she's trying to iron it before bending down and picking up her purse.

Calder hears Miss Kitty chuckle in the background.

"I believe you agreed to go on a date with me," says a deep voice.

"Calder, the lowercase 'D' is the least of your problems now," purrs Miss Kitty.

Calder swings her head toward the dance teacher, willing her to be quiet.

What in the hell? Why is he here? She looks around the room. The mirrors expand her expression like she's in a funhouse of horrors. Where's the fire door? Is that an earthquake? A tremor? Or her soul trying to leave her body through her shoes? Shit. Shit. Shit. Now she's stuck in the dance studio on a date with her friend's ex. A cat's got her tongue. An elephant's on her chest. And a sea breeze is whispering: *You did this to yourself.*

"Calder, this was your idea to meet here, wasn't it?" the deep voice asks.

"I asked GreenseaPhil123 out, not Phil Prescott." She runs her hands through her hair.

"I'm not Phil Prescott, Calder. Surely you know that."

Right, right. Semantics. His last name is Young. Even so, it wasn't part of his profile, so she didn't realize it was the man she's spent a decade-plus sitting across from at back-to-school nights and parent happy hours. She even brought Laura a casserole after he walked out. Yes, it was partly because she wanted to stay in her good graces in case she wanted to put the house on the market—that's not going to happen now—but still. They've always been friends.

She exhales, fighting against her undergarments. How could she be this stupid? She knew meeting was dangerous, but she did not foresee this. And now, her reputation that she's worked to keep impeccable is balancing on a dance floor.

"Your photo was blurry. I could hardly make out the figure walking on the beach. I thought you were some random islander I hadn't met." She makes a mental note to check the prescription for her readers.

"Are there any random islanders you haven't met?" asks Kitty.

Calder glares at her again, urging her to pipe down.

But she's right. There aren't many islanders Calder doesn't know. She's the top realtor on the island. Islanders are her business. But that still doesn't explain this situation. What's that herb she swears improves mental acuity? Whatever it is, she's taking twice as much tomorrow. She let her heart guide her instead of her common sense, and she should've known that always leads to trouble. She should not be on a date with Laura Prescott's baby daddy. She makes people's dreams come true, but apparently, she only creates nightmares for herself. This is going to have to be put in the vault and thrown overboard on her next ferry ride.

She's frozen in the middle of the dance floor even though

her brain's moving a mile a minute. "But wait a second, you knew it was me and still came?" Did he forget that Laura and Calder are friends? Did he forget Fitz took Jo, his daughter, to prom?

"I realized Calderkeystogreensea was you." He smiles with his entire face, showing off his most charming bedside manner. "The idea of a—let's see, how did you say it?—'a night moving to our own beat' enticed GreenseaPhil123." His voice slides over her like it knows exactly where to land.

She picks up her clutch and storms toward the door. "Sorry to waste your time, Phil."

"You can't leave," says Kitty, an octave higher than normal. "You hired us."

"Whatever." She waves her off. "I'll still pay for the lesson." There are fewer consequences if she pays and leaves than if she pays and stays.

"Stay," says Phil.

He inches toward Calder. He's in tailored black dress pants that suggest he didn't let the divorce take his legs with it and a crisp white button-down shirt. He has his tweed sports coat casually draped over his shoulder. He reaches his other hand toward hers, but she retreats to the door like his hand's on fire.

"A little dance won't harm anyone." His long dark lashes pop against his pale brown skin. She blinks her eyes to get rid of the visions of his eyelashes waltzing across her cheek. Damn, what is wrong with her? She shouldn't be this desperate.

A gentle strum of a guitar rings out as Kit ignores her protests and cues up the music. Kitty struts over like she's walking on water. "Let's do this."

Miss Kitty scoops the bag out of Calder's hand and sets it on the table near the door. She walks—more like pushes—Calder toward Phil and takes her left hand and puts it in his right hand. Kitty places Calder's right hand on Phil's shoulder and his left hand on her waist. Against her better judgement, Calder shivers. Her body didn't get the memo that he's off limits.

"Kitty, are you trying to save money by keeping the thermostat so low?"

She should have brought a sweater instead of trying to show off her sexy arms from all her Pilates workouts at The Reformation. But if she's being honest, the quiver is not from the temperature in the room. Every nerve ending in her body is bound and determined to betray her.

"Follow our lead," says Kitty.

Calder watches her reflection in the mirror as she sashays toward Kit. They assume the same position Kitty's placed Calder and Phil in and begin to dance with their hips.

"F-o-r-w-a-r-d, f-o-r-w-a-r-d, forward, forward," Kit croons. "And again."

The warmth from Phil's hand creeps across her entire body. She's a statue. Afraid to move. They're close enough that she can feel his heartbeat, or maybe that's hers, pulsing with reckless abandon.

Phil moves her backward across the floor as he follows Kit's cues. She can't make eye contact. It's like he's the sun during an eclipse and she'll go blind with one look.

"Now pivot. Lead with your hips."

Lost in the words, she's not even sure what he means, but it doesn't matter, because Phil's holding her tight enough that her body has no choice but to follow his. He's carrying all the weight of this lesson while she's treading water in the deep end. And the lifeguard is tall, dark, and a touch too handsome.

"And now," Kit sings the words. "Follow us in the ocho pattern."

And just like that, they're doing figure eights around the studio.

After their next pivot, she squints at Phil. "There's no way this is your first time doing the tango. You've had lessons!" He shakes his head. "Then you watched a lot of Youtube videos!"

"Guilty as charged." His smile has enough wattage to light the entire studio.

Kit stops for a second and looks at them. "And here I thought I was going to have to get the ladder out."

"The ladder?" she asks. "Why on earth would we need a ladder?"

"To get to the next level, of course."

Phil lets out a deep laugh, which makes Kitty giggle, and Calder can't help herself. For a second she forgets what she's doing and where she is.

It's like the first taste of ice cream on a summer day that makes you forget you don't eat dairy. Like turning on the Christmas lights. Sinking into a warm bath. She's missed this. The touch of a man and the spontaneous shared laughter. The joy of being part of a couple, of forgetting whose ex-husband Phil is. Her shoulders relax, and she thinks she stops sweating. She's kept herself so busy pretending that she didn't need any of this, she forgot how good it feels to stop pretending.

"Where are you two off to next?" asks Kit.

Kitty purrs, and reality bites back into view. Going out in public with Phil Young cannot happen.

As if on cue, the song slows, and she drops Phil's hand from hers.

Somehow, between the handcuffs and whips and then Phil showing up, she forgot about her plans to go over to Greenseasy after their lesson.

"Oh, nowhere!" She looks at her wrist, forgetting her watch isn't there. "I have to get home."

Phil puts his hands in his pocket and bounces back and forth on his heels. "It'd be a shame to end this night so early. How about a drive?"

A drive? So they can neck in the woods?

"You'll be like the teenagers," says Kitty.

A maniacal laugh rings through Calder's head, but judging from everyone's faces, it's not only in her mind.

She has got to put an end to this night before they're sending out holiday cards—Brady Bunch style.

"Calder." Phil takes a step toward her. "Get out of your head. It's one night. We're not raising our kids together."

"Well, well...that's right! Because I'm done raising mine, Phil."

Out of the corner of her eye, she notices Miss Kitty nod to Kit, who brings out two glasses of something bubbly. He hands one to Calder and one to Phil. Phil lifts his glass and takes a sip. She grabs hers and drains the glass like she's a college kid playing quarters. Miss Kitty tsks in the corner.

"One more dance, and then we're done," Calder suggests.

She'll live to regret this regardless, so she might as well enjoy Phil's gracious hands splayed across her back for a few more minutes.

no half-assing

Tippy Meadowcroft

Tippy watches Phil leave and Calder turn toward Kit and Miss Kitty, already replaying the footage in her head. Her latest capture is a home run.

She stays tucked behind the bush until the studio lights click off one by one. No one noticed her. Not when Calder arrived, not when the music shifted, not even when Phil leaned in and kissed Calder on the cheek before leaving.

She remained outside behind the shadow of the red velvet curtain. The room was busy: bodies moving, laughter rising and falling, attention pulled in every direction. No one thought to look at the window. No one saw her phone pressed flat against the glass, recording every second. Amanda's tip already has her pulling her weight as a partner.

Tippy's hit with the smell of a home-cooked meal as she blasts through her front door.

"Did you make dinner?" she asks Dave.

"Mom sent me home with a pot pie. I just reheated it," he replies.

Tippy doesn't care who cooked it; it smells divine.

"Where've you been?" He pulls dinner out of the oven. There's something about a man in potholders that does a number on Tippy's stomach.

"Off getting some more footage." She pours herself a glass of chardonnay and pops open a beer for Dave.

"You're taking this thing pretty seriously."

"Dave Sherman, you've known me most of my life. Have you ever known me to half-ass anything?"

"Nope, I have not. I rescind my comment." He serves them each a heaping portion of shepherd's pie.

"Don't you want to know who I was videoing?" Tippy's chomping at the bit to tell him.

He shrugs. "I guess?"

"Calder Cunningham and Phil Young on a date!" Tippy practically spits out her first bite. "You didn't tell me it was hot!"

"You watched me take it out of the oven!"

Tippy's too preoccupied with her latest accomplishment to think about anything else.

"Do you think you should post about Laura's friend and ex-husband dating?" Dave asks her.

"Why not?" Tippy never censors her news because of people's feelings. She posts truths, and people have to deal with the consequences.

"It seems sensitive. That's all."

Hmmph. Tippy snorts. Dave's never understood what she's trying to do. He barely understood the plan for them to fake date, but look what happened. They went from enemies to lovers. Tippy swirls the wine in her glass.

"Trust me. I've got this all under control." Even if she didn't, she will pretend she does.

After dinner, Tippy watches and re-watches Amanda's video of Calder and Phil. This is top-tier content. With the pristine blowout, Blow Bar will be thrilled with their logo placement across the bottom of the video. And the fundraiser bank account will have a nice little sum to go along with it. To top it off, this *Housewives* drama will only drive traffic to the Greensea Geoduck Festival.

Good work, Tippy Meadowcroft! She's done it once again.

call in a tailor

Laura Prescott

Laura reads the text quickly. She can hardly keep track of what's in front of her. The contract for the table and chair rental company has a no seafood slime clause in it, and she's had to reassure them that she will use heavy duty tablecloths. In between all the work for the festival and the job that brings home the bacon, she has no intention of keeping track of Phil's every move, too. Or Calder's.

She puts her phone down and packs up her bag. This committee and the subsequent videos have increased her screen time in a way she's not proud of. She sneaks out the back door of the office and walks over to The Old Owl to take a look at Quinn's license to serve alcohol off premises. At least she'll be able to check another thing of her spreadsheet before she gets home.

The bar's quiet; it's barely happy hour when she arrives. Laura saunters over to her favorite stool. Everything about this place—the sticky floors, the stuffed owl watching over the bar, and especially the owner, Quinn—makes her want to slip off her shoes and hang out.

"These semantics are silly," Quinn says when she sees Laura.

"I know. But you know I'm a rule follower and have to actually see the license."

Laura learned the hard way that paper matters. Renderings look official and promises sound solid, but without city permits and signed approvals, they're just expensive sketches. She's built more than part of her practice cleaning up after people who trusted glossy plans instead of documentation. Since then, she doesn't take anyone at their word. She takes their paperwork.

"You don't trust me?"

Quinn and Laura have been friends for years, and Quinn's mocktails and her smash burger held Laura up during her divorce.

"I trust you implicitly. Now show me the doc."

Quinn runs her hands through her hair and disappears toward the back of the bar while Laura scrolls through her phone and notices a new video pop up. Damn, Tippy sure is busy. Laura presses play. The first thing she notices is Calder's hair. It looks fantastic. Laura makes a note to book an appointment with the blow-dry people, too. Her brow creases as she continues to watch Calder in Miss Kitty's studio. And she lets out a yelp when Phil walks in. So that's what Calder was talking about. Laura pictured a class filled with lots of people. Not this. A private lesson.

"Here you go," Quinn says as she pops out of the back kitchen. "Are you okay?"

Laura hands Quinn her phone. "Watch it for me. And tell me if it's as bad as I think it is."

Quinn takes the phone. Tippy's paired the video with an

electronic Latin instrumental. Quinn's eyes widen and her mouth opens before she sets the phone down.

"Don't watch it now. No need! Who cares about them anyway?" Quinn tries to change the subject, thrusting the liquor license in front of Laura.

"That was Phil on a date with Calder, right?"

"Ummm..." Quinn busies herself wiping the inside of pint glasses with a rag. "It was a dance lesson. Can you consider that a date?"

"What else would you consider it?" Laura fumes.

"I don't know. Maybe Miss Kitty set them up?"

"Were those handcuffs hanging on the table?" Laura resists the urge to pick up the phone again. Self-control has always been her most valuable trait, and she's extra thankful she has some now.

"Yeah, I don't know what was going on in the studio, but it wasn't beginners ballet."

All of Greensea watched the Randolphs and the Lattivers swap partners on the soccer sidelines. At first, everyone stood together at midfield, pretending neutrality. Then, slowly, the crowd divided. Those loyal to Joanie Randolph drifted toward the north goal. Carrie Lattiver's supporters gathered near the south. By halftime, soccer spectators had perfected the dance, switching ends without ever letting the women cross paths. Rumor has it they share holiday dinners these days. Back then, it was still too fresh for that. Laura will not let her family become what they were.

She huffs and gets off the barstool. She's got to get everything under her control and get to the kids before they see this.

"Later," yells Quinn as Laura beelines out of the bar.

———

Laura challenges the 17.5 m.p.h. speed limit on her way home, but unfortunately finds herself behind an older woman driving a blue station wagon going 15 m.p.h. Laura stays on her tail in hopes of urging her to go the actual speed limit. The lady raises her fist at Laura and maintains her slower than turtle speed. As Laura approaches the next stop sign, she veers to the right and takes the back road.

Throwing Betty White in park, she grabs her bag and slams the car door. She runs into the kitchen and starts throwing random food out for an after-school snack. It's the only thing she can think of doing that may erase some of the sting of watching their dad on a date. Sugar makes everything a little bit easier to swallow.

The front door slams, announcing the kids' arrival. George makes his way into the kitchen first.

"Wooey, she is on fire!" he warns.

Jo stomps in and plops her backpack on the island. All hail the arrival of Storm Jo. Meg follows behind her.

"Well? Did you know Dad and Ms. Cunningham went out?" She pulls out a stool at the island while Laura piles a dozen Oreos on a plate.

"You saw the video?" Laura asks, even though it's evident from their reactions they have.

"Yeah, and so did everyone else on Greensea! What the hell?"

"Language, Jo," Laura reprimands. Why she's bothering, she's not sure.

"Do you know how embarrassing it is when people come up to you and tell you your dad got some last night?" Jo asks.

High school is hard enough. Laura can only imagine that people weren't that kind with regard to this. Forget about the ache in her heart; how could Phil and Calder do this to the kids?

"Why did they go on a date with each other? That's lowkey so rude to you." Jo throws her head down on the island.

"Not even lowkey. It's just savage," Meg pipes in.

Laura nods her head and pretends her insides aren't rearranging themselves. They're divorced, so it was bound to happen. To be honest, she didn't really think it would happen so close to home. She curses Phil as she stands at the island of their once family home. Seriously? He had to date someone they've had multiple couples' dinners with over the last decade. Couldn't he cast his net further afield?

"What are you going to do about it?" asks Jo.

Laura has a few ideas of what she'd like to do. Sabotage Calder's next listing. Catfish Phil on Buoy. The rest of her ideas may land her in jail. But she keeps those to herself because she has no doubt Jo would act on them. "Nothing. I can't tell your dad or Calder who they can or cannot date. They're adults."

Laura bites the inside of her lip as she says it and hopes she can at least act like she means what she's saying. She could try to read Phil the riot act, but it would be much like when they divorced. She'd end up standing there with her mouth wide open, listening to his hypnotizing words that slowly rip apart her heart. As a doctor, Phil learned long ago how to share bad news with a comforting smile. Laura spends her days helping people learn the art of compromise, but that was something that was wasted on Phil. Phil has never met a boundary he couldn't charm.

Jo stands up and grabs her phone. "Something has to be done! If you're not going to do anything, I will!"

"Jo!" Laura yells. "Stop! Come back."

Jo slinks back into the kitchen.

"Promise me you won't do anything."

Jo rolls her eyes. "Then you have to."

"I will. We have a committee outing tomorrow. I'll talk to Calder first, and then I'll confront your dad."

When Laura finally gets into bed, she watches the whole video. It only takes a second before the tears hit. How has her life turned into this? Watching her ex dance with someone she considered a friend. A single tear hits her pillow. The anger Laura felt when she first saw the video has been replaced by sadness. How is she going to get through the next few days and the festival? There are at least twenty-seven tasks to complete before the crowds arrive. Mending her heart isn't even on her spreadsheet.

now boarding

Amanda Willows

Amanda Willows is tired, nauseous, and worried she may return to Greensea with fewer passengers than she is leaving with. Calder, Laura, and Tippy—who now considers herself an integral part of the entire festival—made their way to Amanda's car to take the 9:30 ferry boat to Seattle. The women are heading to the rent-or-reuse-it store in the city to find the remaining items they need for the festival.

"I'll ride in front with Amanda." Laura opens the passenger door of the minivan.

Tippy slides the passenger door of the van open, and she and Calder climb in. Amanda inches forward and drives on to the ferry. Out of the corner of her eye, she watches Calder reach her hand up to Laura's shoulder. Laura scooches in her seat as if Calder has cooties and pulls out a yellow legal pad like a general unrolling a battle plan.

"I have the list of things that need to be purchased and rented today. Compostable paper products. Waterproof table coverings. Chairs and tables are confirmed for delivery."

She scans the rest of the page, nodding to herself.

"Okay, let me cross-check this against the spreadsheet."

Her laptop opens with a snap.

"Amanda, where are we on the kid area and volunteers?"

"All set with both." Exhaustion pulls at her voice. The inflatable has been confirmed, and the play area will be set up that day. Amanda sinks back into the headrest after putting the van in park.

"Fantastic. Thank you." Laura squeezes Amanda's forearm before pivoting back to the screen. "Permits are finalized." She taps at the keyboard. "Communications?"

"Check. Check. Check." Calder smiles, unfazed.

Laura pauses. "There are five tasks assigned to you."

"Of course, darling. All done."

Laura doesn't blink. Doesn't type. Doesn't breathe.

The silence stretches long enough for Calder's smile to disappear.

"You don't rip off your clients," Tippy says from the backseat.

Laura turns halfway around. "Excuse me?"

"I'm just saying, you move so fast I assume you prorate for efficiency."

"The festival is a few days away. No time to waste." Laura stares straight ahead.

"I'm going to go use the bathroom. Why don't we all take a break and meet down here when we dock?" Amanda offers, hoping to break the tension hiding itself as getting things done.

The women pile out of the car and go their separate ways. After she uses the restroom, Amanda finds an empty booth at the back of the boat and takes her peanut butter and jelly sandwich out of her bag. Eating little bits helps with the nausea. She only gets through one bite before Tippy finds her and sits in the booth.

"Jeez, it's like we brought along a drill sergeant," says Tippy.

"What'd you expect after she saw the video of the date?"

"She's not even talking about it, though."

The avoidance worries Amanda more than if Calder and Laura had thrown punches in the van. When a lawyer's silent, you know they're getting ready to pounce.

Tippy leans in with her elbows resting on her thighs. "We need to get Buoy to sponsor us."

"Why would they want to after that disastrous date?" Amanda nibbles on her sandwich.

"Any press is good press," quotes Tippy. "And it looks like Calder may have given Phil a bad rating on his date."

"What do you mean?"

"Buoy allows matches to make public comments about people they go out with."

"Really?" Amanda is surprised they allow that to happen.

"Yep. They say it's to promote good behavior. If someone acts like a creep, they're going to get called out for it. Because of the public reporting, Buoy claims to have fifty percent fewer complaints about behavior."

Amanda lifts one shoulder in a half-shrug. "Then I guess it's worth a try—see if they'll sponsor us."

Truth is, she's just trying to get through today. Keeping Tippy happy barely makes the list.

The arrival bell rings, signaling it's time to walk down to the van. Amanda hopes everyone's had a minute to cool off.

The women assume their same seats. Cars inch off the ferry, while everyone stares out different windows. Amanda says a quick thank you to the ferry gods, because the car with the dead battery is behind them and not in front of them. As soon as they're off the boat and on land, Amanda's phone rings. The caller ID on the screen says it's Greensea Elementary.

"Hello?" Amanda picks up the call.

"Amanda?" asks Patricia's familiar voice.

"Yes? Everything okay with Cleo?" Of course, the one time

she goes off island something happens at school. Amanda mentally scrolls through the list of suitable emergency contacts who may be on the island right now.

"Umm...well...depends on how you look at it."

Amanda's jaw clenches. "What! What is it?" Her heart's racing and she wonders if she should pull over.

"I'm afraid to tell you that Cleo has lice."

Tippy cackles in the back seat. Amanda glares at her in the rearview mirror as Tippy pulls her head away from the seat.

"Where?" Amanda's arms start to itch.

"In her hair, sweetie." Patricia laughs.

Amanda exhales in quick succession. "Well, I'm in the city. And so is Thomas. Can she stay in the nurse's office?"

"How about I let her be my helper today? I'll give her a hat from the lost and found and she can sit near me."

Amanda sighs. She should have known better than to leave the island. She pictures poor Cleo walking around in a hat with the word *lice* emblazoned on it. "Thank you, Patricia. I'll be by as soon as we get back."

"What do I do?" Amanda's knuckles turn white on the steering wheel. The last place she wants to be is across the Sound from her child who needs her.

Tippy brushes off her coat. "Which seat does Cleo usually sit in?"

The judgment in Tippy's voice slaps Amanda's cheek. "Yours." Tippy unbuckles and climbs to the third row.

Laura purses her lips. "You're not going to get lice from leather seats." She rubs Amanda's shoulder. "Is this Cleo's first time?"

Amanda nods. Her eyes brimming with tears.

"Each of my kids has had them multiple times," Laura sympathizes.

"Figures," mumbles Tippy. Amanda wishes she would keep her mouth shut.

Laura turns around. "Zip it, Tip."

Calder seizes the moment. "Fern and Fitz have had them too. Greensea Drugs has the all-natural remedy for it."

Lice. Bugs. Amanda doesn't need one more thing to worry about. If Cleo thought Amanda's pregnancy was embarrassing, Amanda can only imagine what she's thinking now.

"Maybe the lice shampoo people will sponsor us!" Tippy chimes in.

"I am not putting this online!" Amanda can imagine all those moms clucking about Cleo. This is bad enough as it is. She harkens back to the years Rose Blackwater called Cleo Little Mismatch because she wore two different socks to school—and it wasn't a mix and match day. What will they call her now?

"You've got this, Amanda. It's not that bad. I'll send you some videos I found online." Laura types away on her phone.

"Strip her bed as soon as you get home," offers Calder.

"Thanks." Amanda takes a couple of deep breaths. The women's supportive words wrap around her like a hug. Even after catching a glimpse of what's behind the curtain at the Willows' house, they're still her friends. She hopes it's not only because they're stuck in a too-small vehicle.

"Let's get ready to build a festival!" Tippy coos as Amanda pulls up in front of a large warehouse.

"Let's do it for the pregnant lady," says Calder.

"Yeah, come on. Let's go," says Laura.

Amanda watches as Calder touches Laura's arm as they walk inside. Laura pulls away. It is going to be a miracle if they make it through this day without throwing punches.

pro tips

Calder Cunningham

Laura studies the list for a second, then tears it clean down the center without looking up. She doesn't ask who wants what. She assigns halves like custody, handing part of it to Amanda and keeping the other half for herself.

Calder snatches the list from Amanda's hand. "You push the cart and follow me."

Calder runs down the aisle, throwing table linens and compostable paper products in the cart. She drops a stack of paper plates on the ground and doesn't even bother bending to pick it up. She drops in a box of forks without even looking at whether they can be recycled.

"Slow down!" Amanda's breathing heavily behind her, trying to catch what she throws in.

Calder stops at the end of the aisle and takes a few deep breaths. Laura has never treated her like a business transaction, and it's scaring her. They didn't speak for a few days after one of Fitz's middle school friends spread a rumor about things Jo's braces got stuck on. But they fixed that with a quick drink at Wine Down. Calder can't even get Laura to make eye contact. Calder is certain that if Laura had to address her directly, it would be "Ms. Cunningham," preferably followed by an invoice.

Amanda and Calder check off all the items on their list with only one break for the bathroom, then head up to the checkout. Laura and Tippy are already there, unloading packages of string lights.

"Assuming you found everything on the list, Amanda?" asks Laura. Laura doesn't look at Calder when she asks.

"Sure did," replies Calder.

Laura tilts her head and glares at Amanda.

"Yes, Calder and I found all the items on your list." Amanda emphasizes Calder's name while Calder drops boxes of utensils on the checkout conveyer.

The women ring up the items and load up the minivan.

"Can I sit in the front this time?" Tippy asks. "I, umm, got a little carsick."

"Nice try. Same seats." Laura walks to the front of the van.

"That's a little childish, don't you think?" Tippy asks.

"It's either that or I'll take a taxi," says Laura, already unlocking her phone as if she would absolutely Uber across the Puget Sound.

"Just get in," Amanda implores. "I'm too tired for you guys to act like children."

The women settle into their seats. Calder, not one to let things fester, decides it's time to open the floodgates.

"Laura, I'm sorry. I didn't know I was meeting Phil. It was a blind date." Calder's voice is measured and calm. Laura keeps her head facing forward.

"Did someone set you up with him?" Tippy asks.

"No, I met him on Buoy." Calder gives Tippy a side-eye.

"Then that's not blind."

Calder wishes Tippy wouldn't stoke the fire right now.

"He's unrecognizable in his profile photo." Calder continues as the air in the van shifts. The only sound is the click of Amanda's turn signal.

Laura turns and inhales through her nose. "That plus his username, GreenseaPhil123, didn't give you any clues?" Her voice is soft. A calm, courtroom Laura is scarier than a hostile Laura.

"He's not the only Phil on Greensea. To be honest, my brain isn't making all the connections lately. I blame my hormones."

"So you're not taking responsibility?" Laura asks.

"No, I do," Calder sighs. "It was all a huge misunderstanding." Calder was only trying to garner a little sympathy. That backfired.

"I certainly didn't think your ex would pursue me on Buoy." If Calder doesn't stand up for herself a little, no one will. She's also terrible at needing to have the last word.

Silence returns to the van. Laura tugs down the visor and picks at something in her eye as she studies her reflection.

"You stayed," Laura says quietly. "That's the part I don't understand." Laura flips the visor back up and turns to Calder. "And if it was truly a blind date on your end and you had no idea Phil was coming, you had plenty of opportunities to leave once he arrived."

Calder rubs her forehead. "In hindsight, I should have left." If Calder could rewind time, she'd have walked out of that dance studio. No—take that back. She'd never have been messaging with a man she didn't know.

"Did you know Tippy was recording you?" Laura asks.

All three women shake their heads.

"No, I had no idea." *My God!* Laura can't think she set this all up. "How did you find out about the date, Tippy?"

Tippy waves her hand. "Don't worry about it!"

Calder makes a silent vow to return to Tippy at a later date.

"Explain to me why you didn't leave," Laura presses.

"I don't know. Miss Kitty and Kit convinced me it was harmless to stay and dance for a bit."

Calder thinks back to that night. It felt like no big deal when it was the four of them in the dance studio. She thought she still controlled the narrative.

Laura whips out her phone and looks at her Notes app.

"You smiled thirteen times. I counted." Laura's not done. "You shivered once, and blushed at least three times. You were easily convinced."

"Geez, Laura. Calder isn't on trial," Amanda says as she drives into the ferry lot.

"It was a mistake. Every single minute was a mistake." Calder looks out the window as she speaks. "Again, I'm sorry. I didn't mean for it to happen."

"At least you gave him a negative review," Tippy adds.

"What are you talking about?" Calder asks. She hasn't so much as opened Buoy since that night.

"The negative review under Phil's profile."

"I didn't write anything on his profile."

Laura turns around in her seat. "Show it to me."

Tippy takes out her phone and hands it to Laura.

Laura reads it out loud. "Pro tip: If your daughter went to prom with her son, it's not a blind date, or an acceptable match." Laura tosses the phone back to Tippy, mumbling the line to herself.

"I did not write that," Calder implores.

The women stay quiet for a second. If Calder didn't write it herself, who did? Is Phil dating multiple island women on Buoy? If he is, that may make Calder's transgression even smaller. But Calder thinks about the statement. It wasn't written by a peer.

"I bet I know who did," says Laura. The ferry crew waves them onto the boat.

"Who?" asks Tippy.

"I'd guess Jo," says Calder.

Laura nods her head. "Bingo!"

The ferry engine runs beneath them, not caring if the women aren't getting along. Calder's stomach twists. Nothing about this situation feels finished.

greensea gazette

Dear Islanders,

The scene is set for the first annual Greensea Geoduck Fest! Only on Greensea could a festival come together in a few weeks' time! It looks like the weather gods are on our side. And not to worry, the town council nixed the idea of fried geoduck lollipops. I mean, really! That would be outrageous! The festival does not need a triple-X rating. Old Man Johnson will be taking people by wagon to and from the designated parking at Island Grocers down to the waterfront. Up first in the covered tent will be the geoduck cooking competition between the infamous Housewives of Greensea Island, followed by the silent auction. Look below for a peek at the must-have items.

A round-trip pass granting immediate access to the next ferry without waiting in line. We're not sure how our committee procured this item, but the ferry system says it is legit.

Amanda Willows will provide one lucky family with 52 loaves of sourdough over the year. Have you seen her bread? Her initials baked into the top of each crisp and airy loaf. Loaves will be delivered warm. I'd advise picking up some of Old Man Johnson's butter and letting it melt away on each piece. Yes, yes. She is pregnant with twins but is committed to continuing the baking regardless of how many mouths she may have to feed. This is a treat you won't want to miss.

Calder Cunningham is auctioning off a one-of-a-kind experience: a swan boat ride in the harbor. A gourmet picnic from Hunter Sorenson—think delicacies from the sea—and bubbles from Grays Bay Winery. It promises to be a night you won't ever forget.

"I'll Handle It" by Laura Prescott will offer five hours of legal consultation. We know Greensea-ers are bent toward legal actions, so we anticipate this package going for a good deal of money.

The Reformation has a group of private Pilates lessons at the studio. The lucky winner will learn to be stretched on the reformer. Trust me, it's worth a million dollars.

And I, GG, am offering a once-in-a-lifetime chance to be GG for a day. I fear we need to diversify the voices we hear on this island. No one likes an echo chamber. The Greensea Gazette will offer the twelve people with the highest bids the opportunity to take over the role for a day.

Dig deep and taste local...from tide to table!
Enjoy!

xoxo,
GG

three, two, one

Tippy Meadowcroft

The sun's barely peeking over the Cascades, sending a few rays into Grays Bay. The tide fills the air with the perfect mix of salty sea. The dew clings to the tabletops as it drips off the festival tents. A wide-eyed seagull circles the area, eyeing its buffet for the day. Tippy hops off Bertha next to the temporary home of Sherman's Shellfish.

"Why are there oysters in there? This is a geoduck festival!" Tippy hovers over one of Dave's body-sized coolers. Her mind begins to short-circuit. Did he harvest the wrong thing?

"Tip, people are going to want more than geoduck. Don't worry. I have plenty of everything."

She hmmphs and marches off. The committee did have to acquiesce and give a little on the theme after they couldn't find any suitable desserts to serve. They decided if it's not geoduck, it has to be Greensea. And that opened up the possibilities. Now, Saltwater Bakeshop is setting up their booth with cut-out shell and ferry cookies. Quinn and The Old Owl have set up a Bloody Ferry—their take on the Bloody Mary—booth. Seas the Scoop dragged a soft serve machine down and is all set to serve saltwater flavored ice cream. Tippy just hopes it tastes better than the real thing.

Booths circle around the tent where the main events of the day will take place—the cooking competition and the auction. Tippy smiles as she looks at the festival. The committee pulled it off in record time. Maybe Mayor Nickerbottom was right to pick Laura, Calder, and Amanda. Although she knows they wouldn't be where they are if not for her.

The committee has kept the price for festival entry low, and each booth has promised to donate a portion of their sales to the Save the Ferry fund.

Painted shells—colored with Earth-safe, biodegradable paint —guide festival-goers from the ferry to the festival grounds. And after the well-timed release of Tippy's *Housewives* video, the attendance should be through the roof. Everyone wants to see if the women can get along.

Tippy scouts the perfect spot in the big tent to set up her tripod. She'll get footage of the rest of the festival throughout the day, but wants to be certain she films all the action between the housewives during the competition.

"Tippy! Tippy!" She turns toward the voice yelling to her across the lawn. Mayor Nickerbottom—dressed in his festival tux and top hat—speed-walks across the grass with a pile of papers in one hand and the other on top of his hat.

"What's up, Mayor?"

"Have you seen the map?" He adjusts his top hat.

She perused it quickly, but it was under Calder's tasks, so she didn't spend much time on it. Calder doesn't miss things. But judging from Mayor Nickerbottom's speed, something must be very wrong.

Tippy bites her bottom lip and shrugs. "Sort of?"

"First of all, I do appreciate that biodegradable paper was

used. Very responsible." He rips the program open and holds it between them. "But we need to talk about the layout."

Tippy stares at the map with a perfectly colored-in festival area in the shape of a geoduck. Of course they went 1000% in on the theme. Impressive. And then there's the walking trail, a cheerful dotted line streaming straight from the ferry dock toward the center of the geoduck.

Tippy's stomach does a slow-motion somersault. No. No. No.

She looks at her watch and fails to think of a reprint miracle. "Festival opens in thirty-eight minutes. There's not enough time to do anything. Let's not hand them out."

"But all the sponsors paid for spots on the back. We can't not hand them out."

He's right. Tippy shrugs her shoulders. "Well, then, we need to hand them out and hope that no one notices." And as she says it, she knows exactly how long that will last. Three minutes or maybe five, because the cell reception is notoriously terrible at the waterfront.

"Meet you at the entrance at ten. I'll film the official opening of the festival."

Mayor Nickerbottom nods and darts off to find the next crisis.

Tippy wanders back to Dave's tent, finding Amanda on the way.

"How are you feeling this morning?" she asks.

"Okay. I have a pocket full of ginger lollipops to stave off the nausea while I'm cooking this stuff."

Perfect. A housewife sucking on a lollipop should add to the entertainment.

"Have you heard from Laura or Calder?" Amanda asks in a whisper.

"Not a word since we went to the city," says Tippy, which

scares her. But it certainly does add to the drama. "Are they here yet?"

"Haven't seen them," answers Amanda.

Tippy scans the festival. It looks like everyone's in their place, ready to open. She checks the entrance. A small crowd is growing at the makeshift gate.

The festival is set to open at 10:07, giving ferry riders enough time to walk off the 9:30 boat and arrive for the opening. Tippy and Amanda walk toward the ribbon. A breathy Laura arrives, dressed in all denim and a beanie. Tippy looks her up and down. Nothing about her says angry. In fact, she looks amazing. Her hair curls perfectly as it peeks out of the beanie. And her makeup is straight off of TikTok.

"You look fab," Tippy says. Thank goodness the negative energy from the other day isn't following her here.

"Thanks. Jo and Meg dressed me for revenge."

Oh. So she is still upset. Revenge chic.

Calder walks up with a tray of coffees. "Morning," she coos. "I brought you each a coffee."

Tippy notices Laura stuff both hands into the front pockets of her jeans.

Calder hands a steaming cup to Amanda. "Decaf."

Another to Tippy.

"Got your order from Troll House." She hands the last to Laura, who shakes her head and steps away.

Before Calder can protest, Mayor Nickerbottom arrives.

"Okay. Let's get this festival opened." He walks to the ribbon with his ceremonial scissors.

Tippy moves to the other side. "First, I need a picture of the committee and the mayor."

Amanda stands to the mayor's right and Laura to his left. Calder sidles up next to Laura.

"Switch with me, Amanda," insists Laura.

Damn. This may be worse than Tippy anticipated, but at least she's getting it all on film.

A slight breeze whips off the trail, carrying a hint of salt and fish parts. The ferry horn bellows across the harbor as Mayor Nickerbottom raises the scissors.

"Three, two, one!" He cuts the ribbon and moves to the side, letting the crowds arrive.

Tippy frames the shot, tripod wobbling slightly, capturing every anxious twitch of the housewives and every first step of the crowd through the damp grass.

the mariana trench

Amanda Willows

"Mom!" Cleo tugs on Amanda's cardigan.

"Mom!" This time Cleo jumps before she can answer. Amanda takes a deep breath. She's a good and patient mom, she reminds herself. "Can I go check out the dig for clams kid zone?"

"May I," corrects Amanda. "And yes, of course."

Although she does wonder why Cleo is asking her permission when Thomas is clearly the one in charge. Amanda has too many other responsibilities today. He's nowhere in sight, so she walks Cleo over, patting herself on the back for thinking of the perfect on-theme kids' activity. A gaggle of high schoolers looking for volunteer hours mans the overgrown sandbox.

"Here you go." A teen with AirPods in their ears hands Cleo a bucket and a shovel.

"Make sure you can see and hear the kids," Amanda says.

She catches Thomas' eye across the grass and does a hand motion indicating Cleo is there before she walks away.

Mrs. Harris clutches Amanda's arm as she passes by. "Fantastic festival, dear. Don't worry about the map. Most people won't even notice how happy the geoduck is."

Mrs. Harris chuckles and wanders away. Amanda opens the map in her hand and gasps. She should have overseen more than the kids' area.

Amanda closes the map, sneaks a notecard out of her overall pockets, and reviews her recipe ideas for the cooking competition. She has no idea what the ingredients will be that she needs to incorporate into her dish—other than geoduck. She's watched oodles of episodes of *Iron Chef* to see if there's any rhyme or reason to how they pair items. She's pretty confident the judges won't require them to use another piece of seafood. Most likely it will be a veggie or fruit and a carb. But leave it to Mayor Nickerbottom to give them a challenge, so really anything is possible. Her brain has already cycled through the worst-case ingredients: tongue, black beans, or, God forbid, red pepper.

Amanda heads toward her minivan for a quick peek at herself in her rearview mirror. Most of her clothes don't let her breathe comfortably anymore. She loosens the straps on her overalls so they don't give her a camel toe or a wedgie. And she's pretty sure her skin is about to break out with a bunch of hormonal acne. At least she's on Tippy's good side with all her help filming the Calder video. Tippy won't do her dirty and make her look bad on camera.

Footsteps crunch on the gravel parking lot, pulling Amanda away from her reflection. Thomas jogs over to her, one hand waving.

"Do we have another pair of shoes for Cleo in the van?" Thomas asks.

Amanda blinks. "Umm...no. I'm afraid to ask why."

"She lost one in the clam zone, and she and George have been digging for it, but it's gone."

"It's a sandbox. Not the Mariana Trench."

"Apparently, Cleo and George were a little overzealous. She's wearing a flip-flop someone had left over from a pedicure."

Eww. Gross. Amanda prides herself on having most things in the car. First-aid kit, check. Snacks, check. Extra underwear, check. Two types of sunscreen, check. But an emergency backup shoe? Probably not.

"Well, I guess she'll have to stay in that." Amanda is too nervous about cooking on stage to deal with a missing shoe. "It will turn up sooner or later. Give the volunteers your cell phone number and have them call you when they find it."

Amanda leaves Thomas at the car and walks back toward the tents, repeating the phrase *I am calm* in her head while the smell of geoduck and fryer oil follows her like a challenge.

geoduck 101

Laura Prescott

Laura buttons and then unbuttons the top button on her shirt. She pops her collar and straightens her beanie. She might as well be walking around naked.

She sucks in some air and holds her head up, forcing a smile as she scans the festival for Calder. She's nowhere in sight, so she walks to the Geoduck Chowder cook-off.

Tureens of chowder, each numbered, line the table, paper cups stacked neatly beside them. Festival-goers ladle small taste tests and shuffle along to the next pot. Laura slips into line and samples chowder number seven. It's warm and creamy, perfectly peppered. She clocks that another option is broth-based, but she's a traditionalist. Still, it feels wrong to vote after trying only one. She lifts the lid on number eight, reaches for a cup, and her arm brushes against another taste-tester.

"Oops! Excuse me!" she says and waits her turn.

"No worries," replies a now-familiar voice.

Laura blushes. "Oh, hi, Owen." Of course she'd bump into

him now. He's balancing two cups of chowder and what looks like a kid-sized hoodie. "I'll try not to make a mess today."

"Good strategy," McHottyPants smiles, eyeing his too-full hands. "We've got a whole bunch of hot soup here."

Laura hasn't seen him since their video went public. This morning her mind is full of details about a million other things, and she's not sure she can add one more thing to her list.

"Have fun today!" She steps away from the chowder.

"Actually, wait! I've been hoping to run into you." McHottyPants takes a step toward her.

"Really?" asks Laura as people bustle around them.

"I thought we could meet on purpose sometime." His blue eyes match the morning sky.

On purpose? The words zip around in her brain.

"Can I take you to dinner next week?" he continues.

A date? Being asked out on a date is the last thing Laura expected today. Not chopping off a finger is all she'd hoped for when the day began.

"If you're not interested, umm, that's fine. I just thought..." Owen stumbles.

"No! No! It's not that." She touches his forearm. "My mind's wrapped up in mollusks with long necks and ex-husbands tangoing with my friends."

"Yeah, sorry. You've got a lot going on. Just wanted to take advantage of seeing you again." His two-dimple smile makes her heart skip.

"Dinner sounds great." She reaches for her phone in her back pocket. "I think if we bump these things together, we can exchange numbers." Her cheeks flame as she realizes what she's saying.

"Something like that," he says and winks. He juggles his chowders and pulls out his phone.

Of course he's smooth. Of course she sounds like she's narrating a tutorial video.

She's suddenly glad she let Jo do her makeup before the festival. Maybe it's the only thing keeping her from looking like she dug up all the geoducks on her own. She straightens her collar, wishing she could also iron her nerves.

Laura attempts a smile. One side of her cheek refuses to cooperate, stuck in a permanent "he likes me" position. Why can't she be normal for five seconds?

"K. Bye." Her elbow is glued to her side, her wave stiff and robotic. She's sure she looks like a parody of herself. God. Maybe online dating really is safer. At least there, no one can see her flinch.

Laura tucks all the awkwardness in her back pocket and beelines over to the main tent. Right now, her only focus should be on the cooking competition. Not dates with cute strangers.

She's studied all the different ways to prepare geoduck—most of them made her gag—and knows that unless all she has to do is reheat the sea creature, there's no way she's in contention to win. The real question is whether she'll be able to keep all her feelings under wraps until after the competition. Her emotional thermostat is on the edge of boiling and she's not sure she can regulate herself.

She gulps down a mouthful of air and looks around the tent. The Fixin' Sixties made makeshift kitchens that sit on the stage for each of the women. They're souped-up camping kitchens, something Laura has never used. There's a stovetop, a sink, a toaster oven contraption, and a workspace. Rudimentary at best, but so are her cooking skills. Name tags label each area. Calder's in the center with the other two on either side of her. Laura scans the tent to see if anyone's watching and then switches Calder and Amanda. It's enough to share a stage; she can't be right next to her.

People start to fill in the seats in front of the stage. Amanda arrives, still sucking a lollipop. Calder comes in, casual as ever.

Laura moves behind her counter, brushing Calder's shoulder as she passes.

She can't stop replaying the video in her head. Phil's hand on the small of Calder's back. Calder leaning into him. Throwing her head back with laughter. It struck every nerve in her being. Yeah, yeah. Calder said it didn't mean anything. But the proof is in the pudding. And the look on Calder's face told a very different story.

Mayor Nickerbottom, still in his Groundhog Day costume, saunters toward the three women.

"Ladies, take a minute to familiarize yourselves with the kitchen. The Fixin' Sixties did a bang-up job for this friendly competition."

Laura may be overthinking, but she hears an emphasis on the word *friendly.*

"Everything looks fantastic, Mayor." Calder slides her hand across the counter.

Insert eye roll.

"Put on your aprons and we'll get ready to reveal our secret ingredients."

Laura tries not to make eye contact with anyone in the audience, and especially not Tippy in the rear corner. Instead, she studies the utensils in her area. Spoons, spatulas, measuring cups, and sharp knives. Laverne, Barb, and Bell walk in, pulling coolers behind them. Each of them stands in front of a station. Bell stands near Laura.

Mayor Nickerbottom glides in front of them. "Welcome to the first annual Geoduck Cooking Competition!"

The crowd lets out a soft cheer.

"Today we have our three—uhm, uhm—housewives, competing against each other. Amanda Willows, Calder Cunningham, and Laura Prescott."

Louder cheers and some applause.

She can do this.

Laura's lips turn up into a small smile.

"Each contestant will create two dishes…"

"Two?" Amanda questions. "I thought we only had to make one!"

Mayor Nickerbottom turns toward her. "Hold on a second. Let me finish explaining." He turns back to the audience and continues. "Bell Meadowcroft, Laverne Nickerbottom, and Barb Sherman will assist as sous chefs."

"Phew," Amanda sighs.

"And now for the moment you've all been waiting for… Without further ado, I'd like to unveil the ingredients the women will have to incorporate into their dishes."

Laura takes a deep breath and rolls her eyes. The moment she's waiting for is climbing into a hot bath after this festival is over.

Mayor Nickerbottom opens a cooler and pulls out an apple and a bunch of greens.

"Is that seaweed?" Calder asks.

"Ding, ding, ding! Ladies, you must make two dishes with the geoduck, and each dish needs to use at least one of the other ingredients."

"You have one hour to complete your assignments! On your marks, get set, GO!" Mayor Nickerbottom waves his top hat.

All the muscles in Laura's body tense. Apples and seaweed. What the hell?

Bell drags the cooler behind her station and touches the small of her back. "We've got this, dear!"

"Obviously you haven't seen me cook." Laura's mastered the art of short-order cooking food that appeals to children, and geoducks do not fall into that category.

"We're going to go for presentation scores." Bell winks.

Of course. Bell Meadowcroft is the most qualified to handle that.

The audience hums with excitement. The air in the tent is

filled with sea life. Laura notices the other women huddled with their partners and grabs Bell's arm. "I've read that geoduck can be used in a sushi roll. Want to try that as one of our dishes?"

"Fantastic idea, doll. Let's use apple in place of cucumber to give it some crunch and wrap it in seaweed."

"What about our second recipe?"

"Go take a look at the pantry and see what other ingredients it's been stocked with."

Laura walks to the back of the tent and checks the freezer and the shelves someone's placed there, filled with all kinds of things. She claims rice for the sushi rolls and then opens the fridge. A box of puff pastry stares at her just as Calder stalks over.

"What do you have there?" Calder peers into Laura's arms.

Laura tucks her items in and huffs at Calder as she walks away.

Ignore her. Stay focused, she reminds herself.

She drops her finds on the counter in front of Bell. "Can we do anything with the puff pastry?"

"Hmmm...what about a pot pie?"

"Oh yeah! Kind of like the one Hunter makes at The Claw?"

Although Laura's certain nothing they make will taste like Hunter's.

"Grand idea! I'll get the rest of the ingredients."

Laura surveys the items when something moves in her periphery. She catches Phil walking into the tent and standing on the side of the stage near Calder. She looks at Calder, whose cheeks redden. How dare he show up here and stand near Calder? Laura's whole body hums with anger. Jo, Meg, and George are seated in the front row to offer Laura support. Wouldn't a decent father be near his children? Every one of her cells pulses.

Laura adds water to a pot of rice as Bell returns with the rest of the items they'll need for their two recipes. The ticking of the timer rings through Laura's ears.

"Why don't you focus on the sushi rolls, and I'll make the pot pie?"

Laura offers up a silent prayer thanking Mayor Nickerbottom for pairing them with a sous chef. She's not sure how'd she manage without Bell.

She peels the apples, lays them on seaweed, and picks up a geoduck. Gray, slimy, and staring at her. Mercifully, Dave Sherman has removed it from the shell. Her stomach quivers.

Calder shuffles over. "May I have the rest of the rice?"

Laura picks up the bag and reaches her arm toward Calder, handing her the rice without turning her head.

"Are you going to act this way toward me forever, Laura? I told you it was an accident."

Laura's whole body starts to warm. Maybe it's a hot flash. It would be just like her to have her first one while she's on stage. She whips off her beanie.

"Mom! You're ruining your look!" Jo cries from the front row.

Laura doesn't care. But removing the beanie doesn't help. She pulls at the neck of her shirt, giving herself some more air.

A hand rests on the small of her back. "Are you doing okay?" asks Bell.

She nods her head, and Bell returns to work, but Calder doesn't move. Laura senses Calder's eyes burrowing into her neck.

"Do you need to take a minute?" Calder asks.

Laura snorts through her nose. If only she were a dragon and could vaporize Calder with fire.

Laura takes a deep breath. *Ignore her*, she tells herself again. But she can't. She glances over as Phil nods his head toward her the way he used to across a crowded sports field, cheering on their kids.

She sets the geoduck on the cutting board and picks up her

knife, raising it to chin level—and freezes, her mind racing before she can act.

"You—" *Chop.* Laura chops the geoduck neck. Bell jumps behind her. Slop flies everywhere.

"—cannot date my ex!" She chops the geoduck again.

Calder yelps and raises her hands in the air. "I'm not! I swear!"

There's a rush of activity behind Laura. Mayor Nickerbottom runs behind the counters and guides Calder back to her station.

"Now, ladies, there will be plenty of time to talk after the contest."

The rubber handle of the knife brands her palm. The blade is wedged into the countertop and the geoduck. Laura's kids sit wide eyed, watching her from the front row. She must get control of herself. But she stands like she's in concrete.

Bell slips off her apron. "Oh dear, it's soaked straight through. It's even in my shoes."

"There's no time for you to change your clothes," Mayor Nickerbottom says with his hands on his hips. He takes off his hat and scratches his head before looking out at the crowd. "I'll have to find you a new sous chef."

Out of the corner of her eye, Laura sees someone walking toward her. "I've got it," says the deep voice that seems to appear whenever she's in crisis. "If you agree to put down the knife."

Something inside of Laura tingles and comes back to life. She sets the knife down and rubs her forehead with the back of her hand. She ekes out a thank-you.

What was she thinking, letting herself get that out of control? She sits in courtrooms with people whose behavior is far less than that.

"What do you have here?" he asks, guiding Laura back to the moment and the task at hand. Like a psychologist moonlighting as a ferry captain.

"Geoduck sushi rolls and a seafood pot pie that seems to have run away in Bell's shoes." Her voice is low and measured.

"Let's trade spots. I'll do the roll, and you make something to go in that dough."

She nods, already easing under his presence, like she's turned on the water for the bath she's been craving and is ready to soak in the bubbles.

He rolls up his sleeves. Forearms flex. Laura's gaze lingers a second too long. She jerks her attention back to the stove. Anything to stop thinking about Calder—and Phil.

Every eye in the tent is focused on Laura and the location of the knives. They're the jury. She needs to convince them she's not so scary. It's simply another day at the office. Deep breaths.

Examining the pot, she sees there's still a bit of the creamy sea creature mixture. Her memories harken back to Jo as an agreeable preteen, making cherry turnovers with the puff pastry. Maybe she can do something like that, but with geoduck. So she gets to work.

"Halfway there!" bellows the mayor.

McHottyPants stands less than two feet from her. Laura can't help but glance over at his back. Her eyes wander down to his jeans, which hug his ass. At least her mind's no longer focused on evil.

"How's your concoction coming?" He catches her gaze.

"Oh, great!" Laura spoons some of the slop into a square of puff pastry. She folds the square in half and sets it on a tray in the toaster oven. There's no way these are going to taste good. The dough will be the only redeeming part.

"How are the rolls?" His strong hands mesmerize her as he rolls the seaweed around the rice into a perfectly shaped tube.

"Perfection." He winks, and Laura can't help but smile. She hopes her knife skills didn't scare him away.

A ripple of whispers runs through the front row. Laura catches Jo's smiling face, then Meg's, too, both clutching programs and giggling. George high-fives a little boy next to him.

Surrounded by seaweed and geoduck slime, it hits her. The real contest isn't the cooking. It's what comes after. The smiling, the smoothing over, the appearing effortless while keeping everything from unraveling. And only some of it is under Laura's control.

i'll do anything alone

Calder Cunningham

Calder spoons the geoduck, rice, and apple mixture into the seaweed cups while Laverne adds vinegar to the geoduck slaw. Calder is certain about several things. First, she'll never cook geoduck again. She's not sure the stench will ever leave her skin. Imagine if she were showing a house and she smelled like this creature. Second, Laura Prescott's knife skills are next level.

Instead of boiling geoduck, she's boiling over with revenge plots for Tippy and Phil. No one makes Calder Cunningham look bad. And they've both done that a little too easily.

Mayor Nickerbottom moves in front of the stage. "Ten more seconds!"

The crowd counts down backward from ten, and cheers rush through the tent as they hit one.

"Step away from your counters."

The women and their sous chefs step back.

"I'd like to introduce you to our celebrity judge." The mayor smiles as Hunter Sorenson emerges.

Calder watches Laura and Amanda exchange looks. At least Calder had one surprise up her sleeve.

Laura lets out an audible breath. "Mayor, really?"

Calder's sure the food is hardly good enough for anyone in the audience, let alone a five-star chef, but at least his presence kicks it up a notch.

"Can't think of anyone more suitable to taste your recipes, Laura!" Mayor Nickerbottom rubs his hands together.

Hunter is better suited for James Beard awards and not moms on a makeshift stage, but Calder knew the star power would help. She's glad he agreed to at least take on the small role of guest judge.

"Hunter will come by, and you may each present your dishes to him. You may begin with Laura."

The ferry captain steps off the stage, leaving Laura front and center without her prince on a white horse. Calder tries to tuck her jealousy under her apron while Laura hands Hunter a plate with what looks like a glorified hot pocket on it.

"You've signed your liability waivers?" Laura asks before he proceeds.

"I won't hold any of you liable." Hunter points to Tippy at the back of the tent. "Tippy has it on film."

He picks it up and tries a bite.

"Mmhmm." He nods his head. His opinion's on lockdown.

"It's a play on your seafood pot pie. It's a geoduck hand pie!" Laura claps.

The crowd laughs. Hunter's eyes grow.

"Laura excels at finger food." Calder can't help herself. The we're-on-her-side laughter from the crowd strikes a nerve, and Calder can't keep her comments in.

Hunter puts the pie down, picks up a piece of sushi, and pops it in his mouth. "Good thing I like finger food." Hunter glares in Calder's direction.

She will never learn to keep her comments to herself. Her

quick wit may do her favors in a real estate negotiation, but it never does in social interactions, especially competitions billed as friendly rivalries.

Hunter approaches Amanda's station.

"I leaned into my Japanese heritage and made a geoduck tempura." Amanda serves Hunter a small plate with a tower of geoduck tempura. It's not fair that she had the TikTok cooking sensation, Barb Sherman, on her side.

Amanda presents her second dish. "A Japanese teppanyaki-style sautéed geoduck and apple sprinkled with seaweed flakes."

Hunter raises an eyebrow and takes a bite. "Thanks, Amanda."

Barb throws an arm around Amanda.

"Last but not least." Calder waves her hand in front of her dishes.

"What do we have here?" Hunter asks.

"Geoduck lettuce cups," Calder replies.

"Ah, more finger food." Hunter pops one in his mouth.

Touché.

"And a geoduck slaw."

Hunter takes a bite. His mouth puckers before he reaches for a glass of water. "A little heavy on the vinegar."

His only comment, and it's not positive.

"Well, there is a lot of bitterness in the air today." Calder laughs it off, but still doesn't get the audience on her side.

Mayor Nickerbottom approaches the stage again. "Well, Hunter, do we have a winner?"

Hunter nods his head. "We do!" Hunter's voice sounds like he's auditioning for a show on the Food Channel. "While each contestant successfully completed the challenge, only one prepared geoduck as it was meant to be."

Calder knows geoduck wasn't meant to sit in a lettuce cup. Was anything meant to, really? But it also wasn't meant to be in a hand pie. As long as Laura doesn't get the top prize, Calder will consider it a win.

"Our winner is Amanda Willows!" Hunter throws his arms in the air.

Amanda's cheeks flush as a small smile appears.

"Fantastic!" Mayor Nickerbottom holds one of Amanda's arms up like she's won a boxing match. The crowd whoops. "We're glad this part is over and we're all still in one piece, enjoy the rest of the festival!"

The tent buzzes with movement and noise. Laura and Amanda's kids run over and hug them while emptiness wraps its arms around Calder. Phil crosses the space to her and lays a hand on her arm, casual enough to look harmless.

"A valiant effort," he says as she recoils from his touch.

Barb walks up and whispers, "Not here, Calder. Give Laura some space. The knives are still out."

Calder crinkles her forehead. Why is she taking the blame when he's the one who approached her?

"Enough, Phil." Calder marches out of the tent without turning around. How did things get so messy? She's been on Buoy for months, and all she did was set up a date—and now she's turned friends into enemies and created a civil war on the island.

She lets the breeze off the bay cool her down and turns her cheeks to the late winter vitamin D. Her aesthetician would admonish her, but at least she's wearing sunscreen.

Shit. A fleeting thought rings through her mind. The auction.

A bullhorn rings through the festival. "Silent auction closing in ten minutes!"

She'd made her entry pre-date with Phil. And now horror fills her mind as she worries he's the one who will try to win it.

Calder races to the auction tent, finding Tippy hovering

around the auction tables. She'll confront her about the videos later. Right now, time is of the essence.

"Tippy!" Calder grabs her arm.

"What's up?"

"We can't let Phil win my auction package."

"Don't we want the highest bidder to win?"

"Of course we do, but it can't be him. You saw Laura with the knife."

Tippy laughs. "Yeah, that's going to make for some good TV." She rubs her hands together.

"Whatever." Calder looks at the auction sheet. Each bidder is identified by a number so there's no way to see who the top bidder is. "I want to bid a thousand dollars more than the highest bidder." Money is the only thing that can get her out of this situation.

"For a date with yourself?"

"You betcha!" It's the only way she can ensure Phil doesn't win.

Tippy points to the table across the tent. "Go talk to Veronica. She's in charge of all of this."

Calder makes a beeline for the auctioneers and explains the situation.

Veronica writes a few things down as she nods her head.

"No problem, C. I've got you."

Relief loosens something in Calder's chest. For the first time all day, she's ahead of the problem instead of chasing it. No awkward dinner. No public bidding war. No Phil smiling like this was all fate.

"Thank you," Calder exhales.

Veronica clips the new bid to the board and moves on to the next item without another thought.

Behind them, Tippy tilts her head, studying the sheet.

"You realize," she says slowly, "if you win, you actually have to do it."

Calder blinks. "Do what?"

"The package." Tippy smiles. "Whatever you promised."

Calder rolls her eyes. "At this point, I'll do anything alone." She turns to leave and runs right into Phil.

"You won your own package?" asks Phil.

"How'd you know?" Wasn't the bidding anonymous?

"Veronica happily let it slip. You didn't have to spend a thousand dollars to get out of dinner with me, Calder." His voice is flat, lacking any of the energy he had at their dance lesson. He runs a hand through his hair. With his turned-down lips, she almost—almost—feels bad.

"Proving I'm loyal to my friends and myself is worth it." Calder heads to her car and her sultry Scot.

biodegradable

Amanda Willows

Amanda watches as the inflatable slide deflates and vendors pack up their tents as she tries to rally the scant clean-up crew.

"Place all the remaining geoduck shells in the crate and put any shoes you find in this bag," she says to the two teenagers left.

Cleaning up is always the loneliest part. Everyone's keen to help set up or work during the event. Those are the glory jobs, when everyone can get public credit for what they're doing. Amanda is used to cleaning up on her own. Doing all the dishes. Mopping floors. Making it look like nothing happened. She's usually the only one left after teacher luncheons, field days, or holiday parties. This is nothing new, but she'd hoped the committee would stick around.

She trudges to each table and picks up the tablecloths, throwing them in a pile on the grass. Gather now. Fold later. Tippy appears out of nowhere to help.

"I thought you left." Amanda's heart skips, knowing she's not the only one here.

"I'm not only in it for the fame. Tippy Meadowcroft always sticks around until the last piece of recycling's picked up."

Amanda had no idea Tippy got it.

"Where are Laura and Calder?" Amanda asks.

"Laura's helping dismantle the kitchens, and Calder doesn't get her hands dirty."

Figures Calder is only in it for the stuff people can see.

"But she did tip the rental company enough that they're willing to fold all the chairs so we don't have to."

Thank goodness for that. Amanda throws another tablecloth on the pile.

"So Buoy agreed to sponsor our last video." Tippy picks up a corner of a tablecloth and hands the other end to Amanda.

"Even after the drama Calder's date caused?" She still doesn't understand why a brand would want to be associated with so much bad publicity. Especially after today.

"I told you, no publicity is bad publicity and their numbers are through the roof. People keep crediting the housewives and GG in the 'how did you hear about us' question."

"Wow! That's amazing." Amanda's a little too tired—and disappointed—to show any more excitement. She was hoping to have a diaper sponsorship instead, but yay for the greater good. They continue folding the pile.

"I'm going to edit the clips and get it posted. But first I need to rehash the day!"

Amanda nods her head. Tippy has a plan for everything.

"Tippy! Tippy!" Mayor Nickerbottom runs toward them with his jacket off and bowtie loosened.

"What now, Mayor?" Tippy's mouth twists.

"The forks are not compostable!" He pulls a white plastic fork out of his pocket and flips it over to show Tippy. "No symbol!"

Amanda's mind rushes back to Calder throwing things in the cart with reckless abandon. She should have checked and double-checked. She knows better than to let something like this slip through the cracks.

"Who cares?" Tippy shrugs. "Throw them away."

Mayor Nickerbottom puts the fork back in his pocket. "There are signs above every compost bin telling people to dispose of them in the bin."

Oh no! Amanda's cleaned up enough events at the school to know what this means.

"Yikes. That's a nightmare. Guess we won't compost this year." Tippy reaches for some string lights.

The mayor clears his throat. "Composting is not an option. It's an obligation."

Laura emerges from the tent, wiping her hands. The women stand like they're in the principal's office, bracing for their punishment.

"You're going you need to separate every fork out of each bin."

"What?" Tippy clutches her chest.

Shit. A shot of guilt punches through Amanda, but she was in survival mode that day. She can't carry the load for every decision.

"Go through the garbage? No way!" Tippy's red hair swishes through the air while she shakes her head.

"Yes way," Mayor Nickerbottom replies. "Wait here."

He scurries off.

"Should we run?" Tippy asks.

"Of course not!" Amanda reprimands. Even though she'd like nothing more than to hop into her bed.

"Text Calder," Laura says. "There's no freaking way she's getting out of this."

Amanda whips out her phone and sends off an S.O.S. text.

Two minutes later, Mayor Nickerbottom appears with rubber gloves and three teenagers carrying the compost bins.

Amanda bites her lip. "I'm not sure my doctor would recommend going through the garbage." She hates not being a team player, but sorting through garbage in her first trimester must be on a list of things to avoid.

"Would any of our doctors say it's the best course?" asks Tippy.

"She's pregnant, Tip." Laura puts on a pair of gloves. "And you've done so much to make sure this day came together."

A half-smile settles on Amanda. Feeling seen is something she's not used to. "We've all worked hard." It's true. She's used to picking up the slack because no one else is doing anything, but that hasn't been the case with these women. For once, cleaning up isn't even that lonely.

"Here." Tippy messes with her phone. "Shine the light on us."

Amanda's happy to have a purpose.

The low rumble of a car approaches. Calder climbs out of her Land Rover in full hazmat suit, mask, and goggles.

"Do you do something in your spare time we don't know about?" Tippy asks Calder, side-eyeing her.

"It's left over from the pandemic."

Laura raises her eyebrows.

"I panicked at the beginning and bought every available supply just in case." Calder removes a plastic grabber from her tote bag and begins extracting forks from the compost.

Laura kneels on the ground, tossing compost items behind her. Garbage splats all over, some accidentally hitting Calder.

"Hey! That's uncalled for!" Calder yells.

"What?" asks Laura.

Amanda toggles the light between the women.

"Throwing garbage at me!"

Laura glares at Calder. "I didn't."

Tippy picks up a handful of discarded shells and throws them at Laura's back. Amanda wishes once again that Tippy wouldn't add fuel to every fire.

"There! Now you've both been hit. Fair and square." Tippy returns to the job in front of her.

"Hardly," says Calder, and throws a compostable bowl at Tippy. "That's for making me look bad in the dirty dancing video."

Calder lifts her arm like she's about to throw something at Laura, the motion big and exaggerated but her hand empty. Laura maneuvers herself away quickly and slips on a bowl filled with melted soft serve, landing on her side on top of the pile.

Amanda takes a step back. This could go sideways.

Calder puts her hands up. "I'm sorry! That was not my intention. I wasn't even going to throw anything at you."

"You seem to repeat that response a lot lately," says Laura. The hazmat suit crinkles as Calder shrugs.

Amanda glances to her left and right, making sure there aren't any weapons nearby. Thank goodness the knives aren't nearby.

Laura sits up. She pulls a shell out of her hair, chucking it to the ground. Wind rustles through the green, and Laura falls to her hands.

No one moves.

Until the silence breaks with Laura's laughter. Tippy looks at Calder. Tippy snorts. Calder guffaws. Amanda's whole body starts to shake with laughter. She lifts the flashlight higher and takes in the scene.

Laura is on her knees in compost. Calder is in an almost spacesuit. Tippy is throwing geoduck shells like confetti. Three of Greensea's finest sitting amongst the garbage.

The inflatable slide behind them finally gives up with a long sigh and collapses into itself.

Amanda laughs harder.

Tomorrow it'll look like nothing ever happened.

"I really am sorry," says Calder, reaching for Laura.

Laura squeezes Calder's hand. "I know," Laura replies. "Phil doesn't deserve either of us."

Calder nods. "What's that saying about putting your friends before guys?"

"Bros before hoes?" answers Tippy quickly like it might be tattooed on her wrist.

"Yeah, that. But make it the female version...and less derogatory." Calder lifts the mask off her face.

"I think you mean sisters before misters," says Laura.

"Yes!" Calder raises an arm of her hazmat costume.

"I wish you'd filmed this," says Calder. "No one would ever believe I'm knee-deep in garbage."

"And that I haven't stabbed you with a plastic fork, and that we're actually laughing together," says Laura.

"I did," replies Tippy. "Video camera's rolling while Amanda's shining the light."

Amanda pulls the phone down to look at it.

She chuckles to herself. Tippy thinks of everything. At least all the invisible work and the ties that bind are etched into permanence. No one films the cleanup. The rinsing. The sorting through what's spoiled and what can be saved. But this is where the real work happens. This is where you find out who stays, who helps when you call, and who doesn't look away when things get dirty or hard.

smash cut

Tippy Meadowcroft

Tippy beams as she rewatches the video.

The geoduck shell logo flickers onto the screen.

(Upbeat music echoes in the background.)

Laura switching spots with Amanda at the festival opening.

One-shoed kids streaking past the lens. Dave Sherman laughing in his waders, shucking oysters into paper boats. Crowds spilling into the tent.

Women bent over steaming pots. Tasting. Chopping. Peeling.

And then Phil in the crowd.

Calder standing over Laura.

(*The music drops out.*)

Laura's eyes widen as she lifts the knife.

Chop.

Geoduck slime flies. Calder retreats.

The tape rewinds to a soundtrack of Mayor Nickerbottom saying, "I see you as the most capable people on the island. It just so happens that you identify as women. Although, I do suspect it is the reason you are so accomplished."

Smash cut to: The women walking down the ferry ramp in a unified line.

Cue giggles at Thin Pines.

Whip pan to: The women working feverishly at The Salty Skein with the generator going.

A montage of greetings with arm touches and hugs between the women.

A full screenshot of the women laughing on top of the garbage.

The screen goes black.

Connections that feel like life preservers,
brought to you by Buoy.

This. This is what it's all about. These women can run an island and their lives—it just may not be pretty.

Tippy uploads the video to her GG channel and pops open her laptop to write her column. She types her first line—*Greensea goes gaga for geoduck*—and stops. The cursor blinks. She types a second line and deletes it. She cracks her knuckles and gets up to feed Bear. When she returns, the blank page screams at her. She's used all her creative energy editing film and left nothing for her day job. Her puns feel stale. Her videos are on fire and her words are a wet blanket. Greensea will survive for twenty-four hours without GG, won't it? Tippy feels her forehead. She must be coming down with something, because she doesn't even care if they miss her words.

beach rentals

Laura Prescott

Rain patters on the roof while the low rumble of a laugh track emanates from the family room. George is up, enjoying free rein of the television without his sisters. The canned laughter sounds too bright for a gray morning.

Laura pulls the covers up to her chin. Her room wears the weather on the inside. But a day without an agenda makes up for the lack of sunshine.

Tippy's recap of the committee's work had her cringing and tearing up. Count the women out when they're emotional, then watch them come back and win. It's the common narrative that's spanned much of her life, but watching it play out on her phone hit different.

She gets up and throws on a hoodie over her pajamas, slips on her slippers, and heads downstairs.

"Morning, buddy." She walks over to the couch and kisses George on the top of the head.

"Morning, Ma!"

"Thanks for cheering me on yesterday!" George was fast asleep by the time Laura got home.

"Anytime! That was nice of Will's dad to help you out again."

"Will's dad?" Her hand freezes short of the coffee pot.

"Yeah. The guy you had the cute-meet with."

"The ferry captain?" A single dad? Laura's dating life is already a cautionary tale.

"Yepperoni!"

"Wait, who's Will?" She remembers the boy who was sitting next to George at the festival. Lots of freckles. Crocs.

"The kid in my class who moved here last year."

Laura doesn't keep track of things like that. She has enough to do to manage her own kids. How is she supposed to remember the addition of a new kid, too? The chocolate milk was probably for Will. It makes so much more sense now. She adds the filter in the coffee pot and pours in the water. "Is Will a nice kid?"

"Sure is! We're planning the summer vacation we're going to take together!"

Laura spills the coffee all over the counter.

"What?"

"Yeah. He's an only kid, so we can share a room when we rent a house at the beach. I'll finally have someone to play with."

Laura's heart goes from pre-trial questioning to sequestered-jury judgment. They haven't even moved to discovery, and George is renting cottages with bunk beds. Oh my gosh. This takes dating to the next level, when kids are not only involved but intertwined. She doesn't even know if they'll go out after her performance last night.

"Will says his dad makes great pancakes! I said you'd be in charge of the s'mores."

"Slow down, speed racer! We only exchanged phone numbers yesterday."

"No worries! Summer vacation is still a couple of months away!"

Laura gulps some of her coffee. George has plans. Laura doesn't even own a suitable swimsuit.

"You can talk to his dad some more when they come over this morning."

Laura spits out her coffee. "What!?"

"I invited Will over for a playdate at ten. Followed your rules: no kids who aren't related by blood in the house before ten a.m."

"Did you forget the first part of the rule? Ask my permission for playdates?"

George laughs. Laura looks at her watch. 9:34, and she's not even wearing a bra.

"You!" She points to George. "Make this kitchen look presentable!"

She darts upstairs to change. Rummaging through her closet, she finds the lounge set she never wears and throws it on. She applies a quick layer of moisturizer and puts her hair in a pony. She dabs a little mascara on her eyes and calls it done. Anything's an improvement from her unhinged behavior with a knife, right? She rode a roller coaster of emotions yesterday—in public. Time to jump into the deep end and see if she left their future on the cutting board.

The doorbell rings at 10 on the dot. Laura's not surprised he's so punctual. He does have to stay on schedule for work. George answers the door, with Laura following close behind.

"Mom, this is Will."

"Hi," she says to the brown-haired boy in front of her. "I'm Laura."

Before he can respond, George grabs his hand and pulls him to the basement rec room, leaving Laura and Owen McHale standing in the foyer.

"Hey." Her voice is a whisper.

"I hope this early morning playdate is okay with you after your big day."

Laura nods.

"I hesitated when the boys asked, but your daughters reassured me that you'd be fine with it."

Laura makes a mental note to remind them of the family rules, too.

"Yeah, yeah. Not a problem." She stands in the foyer, taking him in. He's Sunday casual, too. Dressed in joggers and a Stanford hoodie with a Greensea Island Soccer Club hat. He's not making a move to go. "Come in for a cup of coffee? It's the least I can do after you saved me yesterday."

"That'd be nice." He smiles and follows her to the kitchen.

Owen sits on a stool at the island while Laura makes him a cup of coffee.

"George tells me you moved here last year? What brought you to Greensea?" She holds up the milk, remembering he prefers lattes. He nods.

"Will and I needed a fresh start after his mom left us."

Cue heartstrings as she sets the mug in front of him. What kind of mom leaves her son? Not to mention this dreamy man.

"My aunt lives here. Through my childhood, she regaled me with stories about the ferry rides. I captained boats in the Bay Area, so when this job came up, it was a no-brainer—especially since she's here to help with any babysitting I might need."

"And what do you think of Greensea so far?"

"It's been an auspicious start after I crashed the ferry boat."

Laura laughs and remembers when the boat bumped the piling during the Jac Sherman and Johnny Nickel wedding. Owen fell and ended up with a concussion, but the wedding still went on.

"You might not ever live that down."

A smile tugs at his lips. "I might not, but I'm off probation now, so things seem a little more stable."

It seems so natural, like he belongs in her kitchen, sitting here on a Sunday morning sharing a cup of coffee. Owen's presence is so normal that maybe this afternoon she'll look at rental houses on the coast.

"May I take you to dinner on Tuesday?" Owen's eyes hold hers.

"I'd love that," she squeaks.

"Thanks for the coffee. I'll be back for Will around lunchtime?"

Laura nods, relieved she didn't run this interaction aground before he asked her to dinner.

soft-serve

Amanda Willows

She's twenty-two minutes into an open house screaming match on *Selling Sunset*, and rooting for the woman with the infinity pool because she, too, is one unexpected expense away from bankruptcy, when Tippy calls. Amanda ignores the call. Today is early release day, and she's spent way too much time saving everything but herself lately. She needs a minute.

But Tippy is persistent, and her phone rings again. Amanda sighs and answers it.

"Hey."

"Rent Your Babyhood in Seattle wants to sponsor us!"

Amanda has to hold the phone away from her ear because Tippy's voice is megaphone volume. "But they don't want to give us cash."

"What do they want to give us?" Amanda would take anything, even if it means being Tippy's content for another day.

"Things for your nursery. I wanted to check with you before I answered."

"Yes!" Amanda matches Tippy's voice. "I want all the stuff!"

Having all the nursery stuff supplied will take a huge weight off their shoulders. Amanda didn't keep any of Cleo's baby things, and eight years later they're probably outdated anyway. And plus, now she needs two of everything.

"Fab. I'll answer but I want to float my idea by you first."

The idea's secondary to getting the stuff, but Amanda's ready to listen. "Hit me with it!"

"A gender reveal!"

Flashes of the last island gender reveal and the ensuing power outage blast through Amanda's head. "Ummm...I don't know. I thought you didn't like those."

"I don't, but the internet does. We won't do anything crazy. I spoke with Seas the Scoop and they will do a soft-serve ice cream party for you! They'll use organic, all-natural, dye-free strawberry ice cream if one or both of the twins is a girl and locally foraged blueberry ice cream if you're having any boys!" Tippy is practically frothing at the mouth. "We will hand out mini cones to everyone who comes. No need for utensils, so we'll save ourselves from that fiasco!"

That does sound cute, and Cleo would love it.

"Give me the results when you get them and a guest list and I'll organize everything."

A guest list? Who would Amanda invite? She could invite her PTO board and their kids. People will do anything for free food. But then she risks the "who cares?" comments from people who don't know her.

"Let's just keep it to the housewives."

"Deal!" Tippy chirps, leaving Amanda to wonder if the sponsorship will come with a diaper genie too.

prospects

Calder Cunningham

Calder Cunningham is ready to put the last few weeks behind her. She's pulled her profile from Buoy—no matter how much attention the sponsorship brought her—and is spending quality time with Mr. Darcy.

But first, she's off to show a house on the water to a prospective client for one of the other agents in her office. She hates doing this, not being in control of the information. Her peer, on vacation in Maui, did not do their due diligence, is unreachable, and has only told her to have the house open at 2 p.m. At least she's memorized the house specs.

Calder pulls down the long driveway on this oversized plot of land, passing a stable and a meadow. The house sits due west of Gulls Point—the southernmost tip of the island. The sprawling English Tudor-style home with six bedrooms and nine bathrooms gives off the feeling you've been transported to England.

With little information on the buyer, showing these types of majestic homes rarely turns into a sale. Listings like this attract a

200

lot of lookie-loo attention and few people who can sit with the price tag. Because she wants to be a good coworker, Calder is showing it anyway. But there's no way she'll be serving fresh cookies.

She unlocks the door at 1:55 and does a quick walk-through, making sure nothing's amiss. She turns on all the lights and lights a fire in the fire pit on the deck.

2:00.

2:05.

2:08.

No one. And Calder doesn't do late. She walks out to the deck to turn off the fire pit and lets the sea breeze kiss her cheeks. She looks up at a passing sea plane as it circles Gulls Point. With the Native carvings, it's always a possible tourist spot. This sea plane gets lower with each circle until it lands in front of the house.

Strange. Where is this person going? There's not a good way to traverse up to land unless you don't mind traipsing through blackberry bushes, and there's not a skiff in sight.

The side door of the plane opens, and a man yells up to her.

"Calder Cunningham?" Her name echoes off the waves.

"Yes," she yells back.

"Sebastian Clarke. Your two o'clock." His accent is unmistakably British sounding, like the audiobook crooning in her car.

What on Earth?

"Is there any way up from here?"

"Not unless you plan on scaling a cliff!"

He looks around to the right and the left. "Well, then. Bloody hell. I'll have to reschedule."

Of course he will. "Have your people call my people," she says in jest, and walks back in and turns everything off. She knew this was a waste of her time.

don't forget to
use protection

Laura Prescott

"Ma! He's here!" George yells as Owen's truck pulls into the driveway.

George wastes no time and opens the door as Laura catches her reflection in the foyer mirror and has the disorienting sense she's impersonating someone who goes on dates. Jo did her hair—perfect beach waves—and Meg helped pick her outfit: jeans, black turtleneck, and power boots. Having their buy-in for this date is keeping Laura's stomach from doing extra cartwheels.

"Good evening, Captain," says George.

"Greetings, young man." Owen's voice fills the foyer as Laura slips on her coat and walks toward the door.

Owen hands Laura a bouquet of flowers—a few daffodils and flowering tree branches—wrapped in brown paper. Laura inhales the sweet, clean scent. Eau de new beginnings, she'll call it. She can't remember the last time she received flowers, or any gesture of the sort.

"Thank you," she whispers.

"They're a bit ragtag. Some early spring flowers from our garden."

Laura hands the flowers to Meg. "Will you put them in water? Okay, kids. Girls, make sure to get George to bed at a reasonable time. No questionable shows." She tucks a stray lock of hair behind her ear.

"Stop!" yells Jo. "You're messing it up!"

Laura gives Jo a weak smile and walks toward the truck where Owen stands, holding her door open.

"Don't forget to use protection!" George says as Laura climbs into the truck.

She whips her head around. "George!"

Jo clamps her hand over his mouth. He wiggles free. "What? Seatbelt," he says, wounded. "I meant your seatbelt."

Laura closes the door and hopes Owen gets in quickly.

"Sorry about that," she says, resting her head on the seat.

He laughs, a deep, husky laugh. "Don't forget, I have an eight-year-old as well."

"Everything he does walks the line. I take a deep breath of gratitude when I climb into bed every night that he hasn't fallen onto the dark side."

Owen nods. "Will came home talking about KY jelly the other day."

Laura's face warms. "My fault. George used it in his hair."

"I don't even want to know," Owen says, laughing.

"Yeah, you don't." At least George's comic relief settled Laura's nerves.

"So, where are we headed?" Laura asks.

"Oops, I should have asked you first. Is The Claw okay?"

"Ummm...yeah! Who doesn't love The Claw?" Laura's happy to have a break from Jo's dinner punishment. She's not sure her body can handle another round of pasta with jarred sauce.

"Good."

Owen drives his truck with the seriousness he must drive the ferry. Hands at 10 and 2. Head on a toggle, noting his surroundings. A warmth rises in Laura's heart. She feels safe and cared for —like she might be able to take her eyes off the road—something she hasn't done since before Phil left.

The Claw glows on Main Street like a place where nothing messy has ever happened in public, which is exactly why Laura worries something might tonight—her track record with Owen is not outstanding.

The hostess greets them by name, as if she already knows them, and leads them right to their seat next to the front window. Does he take all his dates here? Owen pulls out her chair facing the window.

"Good evening, Captain, Ms. Prescott," says the server, who appears out of nowhere. "What would you like to drink this evening?"

Owen tilts his hand toward Laura. "Hmmm...may I have a Cosmo?"

"Yes. The Claw's Cosmo?"

"Ummm...I guess? What does that mean?" she asks.

"The Claw's Cosmo is made from vodka and triple sec from Salish Distillery, and hand-pressed island cranberry juice using berries sailed in from a small farm on the mainland."

She forgot how pretentious this restaurant is. She rolls her eyes but orders it anyway. "Sounds fine."

"I'll have the same," says Owen.

Laura licks her lips. If she's not careful, they're going to turn into the Sahara right here at dinner. Owen drums his fingers on the table. Shoot. Is she boring him?

"This is my first date since the divorce," she admits.

"Mine, too." Owen lets out a breath. "I don't know what to do with my hands." He laughs and holds them up.

Laura's face reddens as she notices his capable, lengthy fingers.

The server arrives with their drinks. "Are you ready to order?"

"Shall we start with some oysters?" Owen asks.

"Sounds lovely," she replies. "And I'd love the seafood pie."

"I'll have the same."

"You know you don't have to copy me."

Owen leans in. "I know, but once you've had the seafood pie, how can you possibly have anything else on the menu?"

"I know!" The dough flaked to perfection. The creamy sauce. The delectable bites of salmon and potato. Her mouth waters just thinking about it.

"So has captaining the ferry boat been everything you imagined?"

"Yes...and so much more. Greensea is never boring."

"That it is not!"

It's hard to see outside with the reflection, but a light catches Laura's eye. She squints to get a better look and sees a figure with a camera standing on the sidewalk taking a picture of them.

"OMG!" she yells and stands up.

"What? Is everything okay?"

"Tippy freaking Meadowcroft is filming our date."

Setting her napkin on the table, she barges out of the door.

"Knock it off, Tippy!"

"The fourth wall!" is all she says.

"I don't care about any wall. I did not give you permission to record this."

"Actually, you did. According to the release, I am permitted to record you in public whenever I'd like."

Shit. Of course. But Laura figured it ended with the festival.

"How'd you even know I was here?"

"Well, George mentioned it at school to Cleo, Cleo told Amanda, and Amanda tipped me off."

She rolls her eyes. "Guessing you organized our table in the window?"

"Guilty as charged." She shrugs. "The online fans love this content."

This content is Laura's life, though.

"Tourism is booming because everyone wants to get on the ferry, thanks to you guys. And everyone wants to get a glimpse of the island and maybe its favorite Salty Mamas."

She's never going to get used to that nickname. "The festival is over. Isn't all of this?"

"Nope. Companies loved the Buoy sponsorship so much that I got an offer for sponsorship from a clean makeup company. They're offering a lot of money for you guys to try it. Yesterday a household cleaning company offered to pay for a spot in a video. And that national cookie chain everyone loves wants to send Calder a year's worth of cookies for her open houses. Money is pouring in, Laura."

"Do you think we can agree to keep my love life out of this?"

"No. This is just the content people want to see. Especially after your skirmish at the festival. But we can talk about guidelines at our next meeting—off camera."

"Deal. Owen's release is all squared away?"

"Sure is. Took care of that after your meet-cute."

"Convenient."

"Forward-thinking," Tippy replies.

"Do you have enough footage tonight?" Laura would rather sit with Owen than argue with Tippy, so all her boundaries fall to the sidewalk.

"Sit down and give me one good smile as you take a sip of your drink, and I'll leave you two alone."

Laura walks back into the restaurant. "Sorry about this. Apparently, we've both signed waivers agreeing to this. She'll leave in a second."

Laura plasters the biggest, giggly, full-toothed smile on her face and lifts her Cosmo to her lips and takes a sip. As soon as she sets her drink down, she looks at the window and mouths,

"Beat it." At least she didn't try to get footage of Laura eating an oyster. That belongs on OnlyFans and not the little Youtube channel Tippy has set up.

"How do you feel about all this reality show stuff?" Owen asks.

"Conflicted. We're raising the money we said we would just by living our lives, but it's a huge intrusion."

"The kids okay with it?"

"That's the worst part! They love it and have been egging me on the whole time."

"Of course they have." Owen laughs. "Being in the limelight was something I wasn't expecting on Greensea. But I managed to make myself front-page news right away. Now it's part of everyday life." Owen winks.

Their food arrives, and Laura relaxes when Owen doesn't seem to mind Tippy's cameo in the slightest. If anything, he leans in, amused, unfazed. Dinner unfolds without drama. They talk. They laugh. At one point she forgets to monitor herself entirely, which feels like a small miracle.

By the time the check arrives, she's lighter somehow. Maybe this dating world isn't a gladiator arena after all. Maybe it's just... dinner with a cute guy.

Owen drives her home, the quiet between them comfortable instead of awkward. When he pulls into her driveway, he comes around to open her door, like earlier, like it's not a grand gesture but simply how he moves through the world.

She steps out, aware of the night air, the hum of the engine, the fact that her pulse is suddenly echoing in her ears.

He accompanies her to the front door. There's a half-second where she wonders if she should say something clever, some-thing breezy. But she can't think of anything. Instead, he leans down and presses a gentle kiss to her lips. His lips are soft. And her entire body answers with a warm current that starts at her mouth and travels everywhere at once. For a moment, she forgets every rule she's written for herself.

"I'd like to do this again sometime," he whispers.

"Yeah," she says as she hears Jo yell to George to get away from the window. "Me too." And she slips inside.

"Go, Cougar," George whispers with the confidence of a sports commentator announcing a comeback. Laura gives him a high-five. She can do this.

thank you, next

Calder Cunningham

Calder Cunningham's phone dings with a reminder that says, "Girls." She grabs a meat stick and heads to the front door. Mr. Darcy cries at her feet as she plucks her car keys from the table. She lifts him up and kisses his head.

"I'll be back soon. Promise." She sets the cat down and walks to her car, brushing fur off her sweater. The nip of false spring and the pop of one of her tulips make her smile.

Calder rolls down her window and lets the night air kiss her cheeks.

Laura Prescott

"There's a car honking in the driveway," says Jo as she walks into the kitchen.

"Oh, that must be Calder. She's picking me up for the meeting."

Laura sets the last of the dinner dishes in the sink.

"Will you guys load the dishwasher?"

"Absolutely, Mama-roni, as long as you keep your end of the bargain," says George.

Laura nods. "As long as you tell me what happens on the finale of *Love at Last Resort*." She grabs the compost bin off the counter. She looks at it. For years, she's separated everything because it was the right thing to do. But tonight, she opens the trash can and throws the whole thing in.

———

Amanda Willows

"Just throw all your garbage away when you're done with dinner," Amanda says to Thomas and Cleo.

"Can I keep the box? It's like a little house for the stuffed animal."

Thomas looks to Amanda. "Sure! Just promise to do your reading with Dad."

A horn honks in the driveway.

"Oops! Got to go." Amanda rushes toward the door.

"Wait! You forgot your notebook." Thomas chases after her.

"I think I'll be fine without it tonight." She turns and kisses him.

Laura waves from her window. Amanda glances up at the stars and back at the house. This is actually all she's ever wanted. Family. And friends.

———

Tippy Meadowcroft

Laverne's opened up Greenseasy at The Salty Skein for them tonight. Tippy slips to the back of the yarn shop and tugs the black velvet curtains apart. Inside, a half dozen bistro tables huddle around a marble and brass bar that absolutely does not belong on an island where the dress code is stormy weather chic. This is not Greensea, but Paris, circa 1927. Tippy pulls two tables together, building a command center out of café furniture, just as the others step into the soft-lit secrecy of their meeting space.

"So, Laura, tell us, will there be a second date?" Tippy winks.

Laura's face turns three shades of red, telling Tippy all she needs to know. "Yeah, I hope so."

Calder doesn't look up from her phone. "Jealous?" asks Tippy.

"Not at all." Calder still doesn't move her head.

"What's got your attention, then?" Tippy does not like being ignored.

"Have you guys heard of Sebastian Clarke?" Calder asks.

"The footballer?" Laura replies.

"Yeah, I think so." Calder looks up from her phone.

"How have you not?" Laura asks. "He's George's favorite player. He's always him on that video game."

"What about him?" Tippy cannot imagine why Calder Cunningham would be asking about England's best ex-player.

"He wants me to show him the Gulls Point property."

"Ooh-la-la," says Amanda.

"What?" Tippy drops her phone. "He's moving to Greensea?"

"I guess." Calder shrugs.

This is the last straw. Tippy has lost her edge. How is she the last to know that he's looking here? Her job is to be at the top of her game.

Tippy picks up her phone from the floor while her mind spirals and Mayor Nickerbottom walks in—late as usual.

"After all is said and done, the committee raised forty-six thousand, seven hundred and ninety dollars—just under the required fifty thousand." Mayor Nickerbottom's lips turn down.

The women sigh in unison. They worked so hard and even had sponsors.

"Even with all the sponsorships?" Tippy asks.

"Yes, even with those." He claps his hands. "But! The money you raised was crucial and the viral intrigue you created about the island? That created a surge in tourism the ferry system could not ignore."

"What?!" Tippy did not account for Mayor Nickerbottom becoming a jokester.

"Yes! The ferry system is thrilled with the increase in ridership to Greensea. That coupled with the money you made is, in their eyes, enough to save the galley. The four of you saved it with room to spare."

Cheers erupt in The Salty Skein. Laverne pops out from behind the bar with two bottles—champagne and apple cider. "This calls for a toast!"

"I must admit, I had my doubts about this committee, but we did it," says Laura.

"Somehow we all worked together," Calder beams.

"And I think we even like each other now." Amanda wipes away a tear. "Hormones."

Laverne hands them each a flute.

"To Salty Mamas," Tippy toasts. "The ones who get things done."

The women clink glasses.

"Music to my ears, because..." Mayor Nickerbottom begins, and Tippy holds the camera—and her breath—still. "As you know, the average age of the island has been increasing, and the population of young people has been decreasing."

"Only because of our stellar real estate market," Calder interrupts.

"A good thing that's also become the albatross around our neck." The mayor's mood darkens.

Tippy eyes the mayor. "How so?"

"Enrollment in the schools continues to drop," he points out.

"She's doing her best to help that." Laura points to Amanda.

"Hey! It's a good thing!" Amanda blushes.

Laura holds Amanda's hand in reassurance. "I know." She smiles.

"The school is running on a deficit budget. If someone doesn't help them out, the state will have to step in."

The women gasp around the table. No one wants the state to get involved with anything, let alone their school system.

"But the twins haven't even been born yet." Amanda fans herself.

"All the home values will decrease." Calder wipes her forehead.

"There won't be anyone left to have superfluous disputes." Laura gives half a smile.

"We can all agree this is a major problem, and judging from your grand success, I can think of no better crew to take this issue on."

"But how?" Laura asks.

"Well, that's easy. Keep doing your *Housewives* series and you'll bring people to the island to live and visit. The money you raise from sponsorships can go back into the schools."

"Of course we will," Tippy replies without asking the other women. The mayor needs her, and she won't ignore that.

"I object! It will be too much with my new extra-curricular activities," winks Laura.

"I'm too busy with, umm, the Gulls Point property," says Calder.

"I'm too tired," yawns Amanda, with the only valid excuse.

Tippy looks at each of them. "Remember the fainting, the chopping, the lice? You've all taught me the work never ends and the only way to do it is together!"

She puts out her hand and waits for them to pile theirs on top. Amanda does, then Calder, and finally Laura.

Somewhere out on the water, the ferry horn sounds, and none of them pull their hands away.

greensea gazette

Dear Islanders,

Picture this. The 7:05 ferry glides in on time. Everyone's caffeinated. Ferry pours are more common than rain boots. The Big Dark has packed up and moved south. The city has rescinded its speed limits, and someone has quietly erased every roundabout from existence.

I know. Pipe dreams.

None of it is true, of course. And lately, I've found myself running low on words to describe why.

Since I was a girl perched on my dad's shoulders, I believed the Greensea Gazette would be my crowning achievement. Turns out, writing about this island is one thing. Filming it is another. My camera may be louder than my keyboard.
When I auctioned off twelve spots for brave souls to try my job, I assumed it would be a novelty. A stunt. A way to throw some extra money in the pot. Instead, it feels like perfect timing.

GG isn't over. She's evolving, getting a facelift. While I turn my lens elsewhere, this space will belong to you. The next voices are waiting. Let's decide together who carries it forward.

xoxo,
GG

worth a try
Auditions for GG

Well there...let's give this a go! Howdy, Islanders!

Seas were a little rough the night the galley had to enforce the two-drink-per-customer rule on the boat headed to a concert beloved by the Gen X crowd. Apparently, they can still put it down. Pro tip: we still know it's you, even if you swap golf shirts.

The cafeteria-style food bar is not for sampling. You cannot build a tasting menu out of a tater tot and a spoonful of soup and work your way down the line. Save that strategy for your favorite big-box warehouse on the mainland. Not our galley.

The Salty Mamas have complained about the invisible workload they carry. In the galley, we'd like to gently suggest expanding that vision. There's invisible labor everywhere. Someone wipes the counters. Someone restocks the napkins. Someone scrapes your abandoned cheese cup off the railing. Next time you have a pretzel, wipe up your salt.

xoxo,

~~Esther~~ *(Anonymous Ferry Worker)*

———

Bonjour Islanders,

The Eighth Grade Banquet is the most cherished event on Greensea celebrating our teenagers as they emerge from the arduous task of making it through their first nine years of schooling. Heavens to Betsy, our children deserve this celebration and this chair is glad we've moved beyond whether or not it's a worthy event.

All that being said, the banquet is undergoing some changes this year.

First, the committee will be working in a top-secret location. All members will be required to sign a legally binding confidentiality agreement drafted by our local legal eagle. We will not repeat last year's incident, when the Mardi Gras theme was leaked, publicly panned, and resulted in record-low ticket sales and a competing soirée at Thin Pines.

The PTO has generously agreed to direct a sizable portion of their budget to this one of a kind event. With their generous donation and the private financiers, the sky is the limit. Each decorating captain has carte blanche to transform the weary walls of our school into something unforgettable.

We've even contracted a licensed general contractor to bring in the necessary equipment, sparing us the indignity of scrambling for small machinery permits at the eleventh hour.

Theme park rides will have nothing on this banquet. Mark my words. It will be legendary.

xoxo,

Best Chair Ever

———

Oh sweeties,

Let me share a few things I've learned during my seventy-nine years on this island. I may not be good at reporting gossip, but I'd love to offer some advice.

Greensea is a gorgeous place, but for every manicured landscape, there's a secret to match.

The ferry may run on diesel, but we all know the island runs on women who refuse to let things fall apart. We're the ones who keep it running. Just try not to fall apart yourselves while you're saving it.

It's easy to reinvent yourself on the mainland. There's a suburb and an organization a mile away that's never heard of you. On Greensea, you'd better learn to laugh at yourself, because there's no escaping our water boundaries.

You can't stop gossip on an island any more than you can stop the tide. The best you can do is learn how to float along with it. If it's not the gossip reporter, it's Evelyn who picks up the trash on the side of the road, spotting the cigarette butts you toss out of the car before your driveway. Or Kenji, our mailman, who sees the pink envelopes from the bill collectors. The island runs on gossip.

You've got to choose your enemies carefully. You'll run into them at the grocery store, the ferry, and the town meeting. On Greensea, there's nowhere to hide.

Lastly, honey, if someone's recording you, make sure you say something worth repeating.

Bless your hearts,
Grandma March

let's keep in touch

acknowledgments

With every book, and quite frankly everything I do, my village grows. And the gratitude I feel is overwhelming.

Thank you for loving Greensea. For ferrying over again and again. For finding the magic in this island and its people. It means more than I can ever say.

Thank you to all my favorite local shops for cheering me on. The support I've received from small businesses in the area is unprecedented and means the world. When you shop small, you truly change so many lives. I'd be remiss if I didn't specifically call out my employers, bookstore besties, and friends, Bittina and Kevin, at Away With Words. Becoming a bookseller has fulfilled a lifelong dream, but your friendship and support means the world.

I'm lucky to be part of such a vibrant writing community—at BARN and beyond. Writing can be lonely, but you've made it a shared adventure. With special thanks to my c0-conspirator in all the things, Sarah.

Huge thanks to early readers for all the tweaking, Audrey for editing, and to my mom, Gill, Jenna, and Jen for your ongoing support and sharp proofreading eyes.

Thanks to my girl gang for supporting me on the reformer, the courts, the walking trails, in the sauna, and all around town. I could not do life without you.

Jen—thank you for all your early reading and cover design... amongst all the other fun life things!

Finally, thanks to my fam for being a constant source of

inspiration and support. You guys go above and beyond giving me material. I love all of you more than you'll ever know. A special thanks to Justin for supporting my fictional worlds.

xoxo,
julie

about the author

Julie Farley loves writing books filled with big families, lots of heart, and plenty of laughs. She lives on an island in the Pacific Northwest with her husband and four amazing kids. Julie has a bachelor's degree from the University of Notre Dame and a graduate degree from DePaul University. When she's not busy with her family or writing books, you'll find her watching reality TV...of any sort!

about fog house press

Fog House Press is an independent boutique publishing company offering authors a comprehensive suite of services to ensure their work shines. Our mission is to empower authors to tell their best story by providing full professional publishing services, as well as a host of individual offerings.

also by julie farley

A Greensea Island Adventure Series

Love Songs and Ferry Tales

Cozy Cabins and Ferry Tales

Fake Dates and Ferry Tales

Best Friends and Ferry Tales

The New Ever After Series

Tripped Up Love

The New Ever After

Another Tomorrow

Sunny Valley Girls (Liz Fields and Jess Lynne)

Big Waves Down Under

Holed Up In Jackson

A Fling in the Wild

Behind Two Palms

Greensea Island + Sunny Valley Girls Crossover

All Is Sunny, All Is Green